I would like to dedicate this novel

to my mother, Gail Rinehart.

I graduated college mom.

I know you would be proud of me.

I love you.

Follow me on social media:

Twitter: @Leocollazo43
Instagram: @Leocollazo43
SnapChat: Leothelion2747
Email: Leocollazo43@gmail.com

Use hashtag #OhDonovanNovel
Post about my novel!

Oh Donovan

Leonardo Collazo

"Depression is the inability to construct a future."
\- Rollo May

*"A man devoid of hope and conscious of being so has
ceased to belong to the future."*
\- Albert Camus

*"When you feel the last bit of breath leaving their body,
you're looking into their eyes. A person in that
situation is God!"*
\- Ted Bundy

*"That's when I realized that death was the
ultimate thrill."*
\- John Wayne Gacy

1

I wake up some days expecting a better life. I guess it's because I live an uneventful one. A life without purpose. A life cannot be purposeful when the top activity during your day besides breathing is masturbation.

I like to live in my head. I feel safe there. I'm not very social. I'm internally social. My thoughts are my friends. I have very few human friends. I see them occasionally; rarely. I could live without them. I need new friends.

I hate Sundays.

Today is Sunday.

It's either the last day of the week or the first. It consists of no particular order; waking up, bathing, eating breakfast, going to church, eating more, watching TV, spending time with family, and getting ready for a forty plus hour work week for the average adult.

Try not to vomit.

I don't want the average life. I don't want my life either. A crossroads has been built in my head, my thoughts. I think I should talk to someone. I think it's stressing me out.

My room is my place of comfort. Lately it feels like a prison. I live in my room. I'm stuck here. This house is a prison. My life is literally contained in this house.

I need to go out more.

My life is falling apart. I hope not. How can something fall apart when something isn't there? Life is weird. My life is weird. I hope life isn't weird. There has to be more to life.

Please let there be.

I've been panicking lately. Not panic attacks. I'm not crazy. Nothing is wrong with me. I just have to find a better life. I need to invest in a life manual. Life can't consist of being a young twenty-something year old adult still living with their mother. With no job. No responsibilities. Mother still providing everything for me.

I want purpose. I want meaning.

I ran out of both.

I'm pathetic.

I feel my heart pumping in my chest more and more when I socialize with my thoughts. I don't like it. I never used to notice my heart pumping. Do my thoughts disturb me? Is the realization of my life, my purpose, scaring the shit out of me? I really hope not.

Relax. Breath. Relax.

My mother's voice loudly echoes into my room. She wants my attention.

You have it. I need a break from my thoughts.

"The weather looks beautiful outside."

I look outside of my window. "No thank you." If I was a vampire I'll hiss in disgust at the brightness. Fortunately, I'm not a vampire.

"I'm heading out. Need anything?"

"Chips." All I eat are chips and junk. All I eat are chips and *fucking junk!*

Relax.

"What are your plans for today?"

Masturbating multiple times. I'm fucking pathetic. My life is pathetic. "Job searching online."

"Ok Donnie. I'll see you later."

"Donovan. It's Donovan."

Silence.

It's just my mother and I in this house. My room is upstairs, while her room is downstairs on the opposite side of the house. She's fortunate that her room isn't directly under mine for obvious reasons. I masturbate too much and

I'd rather not use headphones.

Summertime is here and I don't have an air conditioner in my room. The musk and funk can get pretty unbearable in here, but I do nothing to fix it. I know how to.

Clean up your room Donovan.

I choose not to. I have the power to but I choose not to.

We live in a small quiet town. An uneventful town. That sounds kinda like my life. Very similar. Could that be the problem? I don't want to know.

I have nowhere to go.

A few crimes happen every once in a while. This town isn't built for a higher class of people. There is nothing here. A park or two. Plenty of schools. You'll love it here if you like schools. No malls or clubs. Two bars. This town is built for people that need two or more jobs to survive. A couple thousand people live here. Nobody famous. Nobody or nothing to brag about. Good luck finding it on a state map.

I guess I'll consider myself a bum. I guess that's a good description. I don't like that characteristic of myself. I guess I use that description because I'm in my mid-twenties still living with my mother. Or it's because I don't work. Or it's because I sleep in until three in the afternoon on most days. Or it's because I haven't cleaned my room in years and it has a sinister smell to it. Or it's because I didn't go to college after high school like friends and former classmates after graduation, then studying hours upon hours upon hours to be doctors and lawyers because mommy and daddy wanted the best for me.

I'll pass.

But that's what life wants from me. I don't want that. I don't want my life. I don't know what type of life I want. Gotta figure it out Donovan.

My mother always told me a father would have been really important for me growing up. Said that's why I like to keep to myself. She says fathers give boys guidance and help them become men and become wise. Something called a dad is what she said I needed in life. What the fuck is a dad? My vocabulary is limited. I didn't attend college.

I sometimes hear my mother cry at night begging God to save me.

Do I need to be saved?

Please God. Come save me. My thoughts make me feel weird. My life isn't ideal. I'll like a new one. My heart pounds too much when I think about my life. I get lightheaded. Is that normal?

Hello?

No reply.

Give him time Donovan.

How much time do I have?

Stop pounding, heart. Stop getting lightheaded, head. Be regular. Like… like… like y'all were a few days ago. Was it days or weeks ago? Months maybe? The answer is somewhere in my head. Why can't I find it?

Stop fucking thinking about it. Breathe.

My life is boring. I need a new one. I keep thinking that. I've been feeling miserable lately, like I'm wasting my time on this planet. Probably some phase people my age go through. I just need a pill to fix it. My mother will set an appointment. My mother does everything for me. Is that how it should be? No. I don't know.

Depression?

Nonsense!

Stress?

No Donovan.

I just sit in my room all day and play with myself. This phase should be over soon.

What a life.

I hate my life.

No I don't. I just hate parts of it.

That is nothing to be depressed about. Everyone hates parts of their life. My mother works two minimum wage jobs. Pretty sure she hates that. You have nothing to be stressed about. You literally have nothing. Breathe Donovan. You just need to slay the dragon once or twice. Relieve the stress. That's what you need. Calm down. Just calm down.

Why won't my heart stop pounding? I don't like this feeling.

Lately my body's been feeling foreign.

I turn my computer on or what I like to call cumputer and wait for it to start up. My computer's only purpose is literally to find things that make me cum. Videos that make sperm and semen ejaculate from my penis. My computer hates its life. I definitely know that. The cumputer takes a while to start up.

Porn can do damage to these things. All I wish to do when I wanna watch porn is beat off and watch porn, but that's not what you're going to get when you're like myself and a million other guys watching the free stuff. Mr. and Mrs. Pop-ups like to stop by. Their children like to visit. And their children's children too.

Pop-ups are a family in my life, my pathetic little world. They're one annoying family. They visit me every single time I want to watch porn. I murder them with mouse clicks. They avenge their death. Their ghosts haunt me with viruses and junk.

That explains the slowness on my computer.

I'm tired of watching porn. I watch it every day. It's not exciting anymore. It's boring. My life is boring. I watch groups of people be sexually active for a duration of time. I want some action. My hands have to hate me by now. We have an awkward relationship. I sometimes call my left hand Handrea. I haven't named my right one. They're slaves to my penis. What a life.

I don't like this feeling I'm feeling. It feels like I'm spacing out, my mind is leaving my body. I should watch some TV. Something good should be on.

Please be.

Relax. Breathe. Breathing slows down your heart rate

Donovan. I learned that in health class or gym class. I don't remember. I should.

Just breathe.

I turn the TV on. I start flicking through channels. I take deep breaths. Relax. There is always a slasher flick on, even on a Sunday of all days. I like those. They keep me interested. I cannot move my eyes away from looking at the TV when there is a slasher on. A slasher gets my full attention. I flip through the channels and to my surprise there is none. Not even the low budget ones with too much blood. I need an escape from my thoughts.

Just watch some reality TV.

Hell no. I don't want to watch shit.

Today sucks. I hate today. Think of something else to do. Why can't I think of something else? Something else has to be in my mind. Think Donovan.

What the fuck is going on?

Calm down Donovan. Stop panicking! I'm starting to sweat. Oh man, you're sweating now. My heart is pounding. Is this a panic attack? Nonsense! I'm feeling light headed. Stop it body! I feel healthy. I did feel healthy. I haven't been running. I should start running. Too much junk food Donovan. God damn I think I'm having a panic attack! Why am I struggling to breathe? *Breathe GODDAMMIT!* Calm down Donovan! I just need to take a walk. I don't take walks. I need to get out more. This is not good. Something is wrong. I'm starting to shake. I need to sit down. Why am I standing up? Just sit down. Relax. I keep telling myself to relax but it isn't working. Why won't my body listen? I'm in my place of peace, but I'm far from being at peace. I don't know what I am. I need to get out of this house because in here is not what I'm in need of. Just take the walk Donovan! Breathe dammit!

I hurry downstairs into the kitchen where the door to my freedom resides. Mother isn't back yet. She takes forever to do anything. Focus Donovan. I'm starting to see spots in my vision. You're burning up! I feel sick. Why am I sick? Drink some water. I turn the sink on. Cool yourself down Donovan. My throat isn't working properly. It's struggling to swallow the water. Failing actually. *Oh God!* I need to get out of this fucking house. I unlock the door so I can escape this place. There has to be something out there for me!

Save me God.

All I'm wearing are a pair of fucking boxer briefs. God dammit Donovan! Pull yourself together! I'm shaking even more. My jaw trembles. White spots invade my view. Stop it! Take control of yourself Donovan.

I'm losing control.

I dash for my room. I need clothes. But I need fresh air. Crossroads. No. Stop it.

Think.

Can't.

Almost to my room.

Clothes.

Fresh air.

Everything becomes distant.

No!

Come back.

Darkness becomes my world.

2

Darkness is still surrounding me when I become conscious. This is a new darkness. It's nighttime.

I'm hungry.

My nose is throbbing in pain. I must have collapsed flat on my face. How long have I been down here? I attempt to get up off the ground, but my left arm is stuck beneath my body. My arm is in an unnatural position. As I get my arm free I notice it's limp. I need to get blood back into my arm before I get up. I notice that the TV is on downstairs and awfully loud at that.

Mother is finally home.

I'm surprised I didn't notice the sound this whole time. What time is it? I scan around the darkness. My stomach is growling. Moonlight is shining on something shiny on my bed. A bag it seems. A bag of chips. So mother has been in my room. So mother has seen me down here. So why didn't mother wake Donovan up? It doesn't matter. My arm is good now. I get up and head towards the bathroom.

I need something to eat. I walk back to my room and pick up the chips. Salt and vinegar? I toss them near the trash can and walk to the bathroom.

Not much damage is done to my nose as I inspect it in the bathroom mirror. Just some bruising to the tip of it. Thanks hardwood floor. I look at the rest of my face. The face of a young adult with no future. I have bags under my eyes from years stuck staring at screens. I look old for my age. I look like I'm thirty, but I'm still in my twenties.

I see no success when I look in the mirror. No millionaire is looking back at me. No successful businessman. No businessman at all. No doctor. No actor. Maybe a trash man. Maybe a janitor. Maybe a homeless man. I'm headed for their lifestyle. I see no advancement in my future.

I'm nothing. I'm going to die a bum. I've earned it. I haven't fought against it. Die a bum you bum.

You won world.

I'm waiting for the panic to attack my body as it did earlier, but nothing. I guess you finally accepted it Donovan. No need to panic over the inevitable.

I walk downstairs to eat dinner. My mother mumbles something foreign to me, but I ignore it. I'm starving. The menu tonight is leftovers. Thanks. I eat then head back upstairs to lay in bed and stare into the darkness.

I feel no need to masturbate, which is odd. Very odd. I don't remember the last time I didn't wrestle the cobra for a whole day before. Playing with my penis won't change my mood. It won't change my lifestyle. Years of doing it didn't change me and I highly doubt doing it today will. Lately it has done no justice to satisfy me.

Just sleep Donovan.

Yeah, just sleep. Maybe I'll be back to the old Donovan in the morning.

I lay in bed. Exhausted, but not tired. I lay and I lay and I lay in the darkness. What time is it? I was wondering about the time earlier. Where is my phone? I search the covers with my hands and find my cell phone. It is the morning already. Two hours into the morning at that. It's Monday. I close my eyes, but have no success falling asleep. I decide to just stare into the darkness until I'm asleep. Footsteps become a new sound in my head. My mother is walking upstairs. Hello mother. What does she want?

"Hey Donnie, you awake?" she asks yawning. My mother flicks the light switch on. She must be worried about me. She rarely visits the second floor.

This is her second visit.

"It's Donovan."

"Find any jobs online?"

"Plenty." None. I forgot.

"Where?" She insists to know. You can tell from her tone of voice, expression on her face, and hand on her hip. Typical mother.

"It's like two in the morning."

"Just tell me a few then."

"Why didn't you wake me up when you brought the chips upstairs?"

"Because I didn't see no empty pill bottles on the floor. No blood. You were breathing. Snoring quite a bit. But what I did see was naked women all on your laptop. So I knew everything was ok."

I left my browser up?

Wow Donovan.

I didn't respond to her statement. There was no need.

"Well you have a good night Donnie. I love you son."

"Donovan."

She leaves the room without turning the light off.

I throw whatever clothing I can grab near me within arm's length in hopes of turning that light off. I wasn't getting up. I succeeded once I got a hold of a hoodie at the edge of my bed.

Now Donovan can sleep. If only it was as easy as saying it. It'll be nice if I could just fall asleep instantly like flicking a switch to turn a light off. Just flick my brain off, my thoughts.

They sometimes keep me awake.

I'm wide awake.

Damn. More staring into the darkness for you, Donovan. As I'm laying here I wonder how white and infested this room would be if my ceiling light was actually a black light. Too white I assume.

I fall asleep sometime in the near future.

3

The next couple of days were mainly spent in my room lying in my bed to vegetate. I rarely got out of bed and when I did it was only to eat and drink and then release the waste the food or liquid became. My bed became my coffin. But I wasn't dying. I'm just miserable. I should die. Try something new.

Death.

Die Donovan.

Life isn't worth it.

Life sucks.

I tried waxing my pole, but he won't even salute me no more. Poor penis. Even my body is giving up on me.

Pathetic Donovan.

Poor pathetic me.

Today I'm going to try something new. I'm actually gonna get out of bed and go to a place that is not my house. Wow Donovan. Good for you. I head into the bathroom.

I get into the bathroom and it smells like shit. I forgot to flush last time I used the toilet. It can wait because I have to go again. As I'm releasing my bodily waste I check the weather on my phone. It's going to be in the high nineties today and it's only May. This summer is going to be hell. It's so relaxing using the bathroom. You get to be alone and just think about whatever your little brain desires, however, my thoughts have been nothing but negative. I thought they were my friends?

Not all the time.

I decide to reminisce on my past. I decide to spend my time spent on this toilet to think about this one time I got caught taking a picture of one of my former teachers, Mrs. Revis.

Mrs. Revis was my favorite teacher in high school and it wasn't because of her personality or friendliness, it was because of her body. She has a body of an ideal milf. High school boys love milfs. She has the big boobs, the big butt, long legs, blonde hair, sexy smile, mature sexy face, and she used to give you the look that said *fuck me right now* during calculus or so I use to think. At least that's how I interpreted that look.

It was a warm summer day when I saw her. It was the summer after I graduated school and I was at the mall. I tried countless of times to take pictures of her during class whether she had on revealing clothes or bent over to help a fellow student in front of me. Every time I had the perfect picture to take on my phone, there always was this girl, Marla, this ugly fat chick with black hair, who gave me this look that said *take that picture, I dare you, and I'm telling as soon as you do!*

Stupid Bitch.

Marla the bitch.

I had chances upon chances to take pictures that would make students hide in the bathroom to fondle themselves to perfect images of Mrs. Revis but no, Marla wanted to be a fat bitch and snitch if I did. Those could have been billion dollar pictures. Maybe not a billion dollars but I could have made something awfully nice off of them.

I was walking around the mall looking for the perfect picture to take of big booties and big boobies. I wasn't having much success and I decided to go to the food court because girls with big accessories like to eat. I was young and dumb and that's how I thought.

I still think like that.

I found a few to take, but none were really amazing. Just

a few of women showing a good amount of cleavage and okay butts in tight jeans. Then across the food court I saw her. The one that always got away. The one that Marla the bitch always stopped me from getting, Mrs. Revis.

Finally.

I couldn't believe it. There she was, across from the food court, walking out of some clothing store, holding a bag probably full of purchases of fancy thongs and lingerie, wearing these purple leggings that begged for attention with a pretty black tank top. I remember I just wanted to explode inside my cargo shorts. I wasn't going to waste this opportunity. A picture of Mrs. Revis will become a part of my cell phone collection.

I started following her, but kept a good distance away. I didn't need to be too close since the megapixels on my phone gave me quality photos. I started to take a few sample shots, none too erection worthy, so I was guaranteed to bring home some photos of Mrs. Revis finally.

Yes!

Now if only the mall people will just stop getting in the way of her plump, perfect backside, I will at last have amazing photos of the sexy Mrs. Revis. I kept having this feeling that Marla was going to pop out of nowhere and give that stupid look that used to ruin perfect opportunities.

Someone did.

After getting amazing photos of her bottom in those purple leggings that fit so perfectly like they were made specifically for her, I decided it was time to take some photos of her lovely breasts. She was blessed.

I got a good distance in front of her and posted up next to a tree. I don't know why some designers put trees inside of malls. I personally think it's tacky. The camera becomes focused and zoomed up on her breasts. I didn't make it look too obvious. I acted like I was busy playing a game on my phone. When I found the ideal opportunity to take a picture of her lovely breasts I feel a hand grab my shoulder.

Rather hard if I remember well.

I turn around and it's a mall rent-a-cop and he's an old one too. They believe they're actually a cop and mean something to society.

"What do you think you're doing?"

"Uh...uh..." I should have said shut up old man.

"Don't play dumb with me boy. You're taking pictures of that pretty lady over there."

"Are you serious? Don't you have more important stuff to worry about?"

"Give me that damn phone boy!"

He grabs for my phone like I'm going to allow this old geezer to take it. I snatch my phone away from his grasp and start sprinting for the closest exit.

He doesn't follow after me.

I get on the next bus that heads home. I couldn't believe I got caught by a rent-a-cop. They do absolutely nothing while they work. All I see them do are riding around on their Segway's with sticks shoved up their asses. Stupid security guards. I only got a few good pictures of Mrs. Revis's bottom and none of her front accessories.

I was so disappointed that whole ride home.

I at least had some pictures though.

Following my number two and reminiscing of my failure way back when, I take a cold shower. I try to enjoy the coolness of the water since today is not going to be cool at all. My penis rises momentarily, but then falls back down. I thought I felt a tear roll down my eye as he went limp. Probably just water. The climax has a distinct feeling when you are taking a shower. I personally enjoy the feeling.

I walk to the bus stop down my street. Bus arrives ten minutes late. Typical public transportation. The lady next to me smells of piss. How long before I become her? The air conditioner on the bus is currently not working. The heat intensifies the piss smell. I thought of moving my seat, but I didn't see any free ones.

As I was looking around I see someone familiar. A face I hope whose eyes don't notice my face. Unfortunately the eyes notice me. The face belonged to Brian.

I don't like Brian.

Brian had to be done with high school by now. I graduated four to five years ago. Sometimes I don't remember. Is it that I don't remember or don't care?

Both.

He wasn't alone. I guess he's with his boys. They were smoking the plant of many names. Pot, weed, marijuana, broccoli, grass, reefer, skunk, bud, chronic, and many others. People that smoke get really creative.

His friends and him are babbling a lot of random stuff which I notice people do when they smoke pot. It was disappointing to see. Last time I saw him he was smoking cigarettes. He must be moving up in the world.

He walks over to my seat.

"Want to hit it Donnie?"

I laugh surprisingly, slightly and politely refuse with a wave of my hand.

"Still being a good boy I see. Your mom should be proud. By the way how's she doing? She still sexy Donnie?"

I didn't respond. He knows I hate when people call me that.

We took the same bus to school my senior year of high school. Stood at the same bus stop too. Brian is one annoying individual. Every day on the bus Brian thought it was his duty to get on my nerves. His life's purpose. It's a challenge to be able to do so, but Brian knew how to push all the correct buttons. He would yap in my ear and mess with me and brag about the girls he fucked and how he could help provide me with some pussy, as he used to say. I never figured out how he knew I never used to get any.

Must have been written on my face or something.

"Want to know my body count?" Brian asked.

"Body count?"

"Girls I fucked."

Lady next to me looks in disgust at Brian. I can't blame her. I'm disgusted at both of them. Same old Brian. "I'll pass."

"I was asking because I'm at an odd number. You think your mom will let me become even? You know I've always wanted to."

This is why I don't go outside.

He snickers.

Why did God create people like Brian? I've always wondered that. To me that was a waste of God's time. I guess every one he creates can't be respectful.

"I have a question for you Brian."

"You didn't answer mine Donnie."

It's Donovan. "That's because I'm not answering your question. My question is why are you an asshole?"

He laughs. "What?"

"Why?"

"Because I heard your mom loves eating ass." More laughter leaves his mouth. His friends join in with laughter.

"That's your best answer?"

"Yeah."

I just stare at him.

Brian goes back to his seat. This piss smell is getting unbearable. Every time someone gets off the bus, another passenger gets on. Today is just not my day. When is this piss lady going to get off the bus? A few minutes pass and Brian decides to come annoy me some more.

"How is your ass doing?"

"What?" I'm confused.

"I'm asking cause I heard you got ass cancer by getting fucked in the ass all the time in school."

His friends laugh in the background.

"Why do you talk to me Brian? I'm not one of your friends."

"Cause you're easy to mess with, and I'm trying to fuck

your mom tonight. Help me out."

More laughs from the peanut gallery in the back.

I'm easy to mess with? I just smile at him.

I'm pathetic. I'm nothing and now I'm easy to mess with. The list continues.

Why did God make idiots? Nobody will ever know until they make it to heaven. I think he made idiots for people to feel bad for them. I think God made Brian for me to beat on this sunny afternoon.

No Donovan. You're nothing. Stay nothing. Stay hidden in your shell. You should have stayed in the house.

I think I should do something. Today is a new day.

Brian gets off the bus at one of the stops before the mall. His friends stay on the bus. I follow him. I will not be at the mall this afternoon. He doesn't notice that I got off with him.

What am I doing?

I'm not sure.

I follow Brian for some time. He walks into an alleyway. I pick up a gray rock the size of a golf ball.

What am I doing?

I throw the rock at the back of his red shirt.

I want to hurt him.

I want to annoy him.

He turns around quickly, surprised. I charge at him. His ugly brown nose is right there, and I strike him with my right hand.

Brian hits the ground hard.

Whoah.

I did that.

"AHHHHHHHHH! My fucking nose. My fucking nose is broken. IT'S BROKEN!" It better be fucking broken.

I grow angry.

No more annoying Donovan. Take control Donovan.

Take control of your life.

Poor little Brian is lying there with a broken nose. It does look broken. The dorsum of his nose is bent. Thank God for high school health class for teaching me what a dorsum is. Blood is starting to leak from his right nostril. He asked for a broken nose.

When he said *I'm trying to fuck your mom tonight* he really meant *Donovan I want you to break my nose because my name is Brian and I'm an idiot.* Yeah that is what Brian wanted me to do. He just begged for me to do it the whole bus ride.

That is my interpretation.

I'm tired of being nothing.

I think he wants me to hit him a few more times. He won't be quiet. Brian's nose is starting to turn a dark purple. It sucks to be Brian's nose right now.

"Oh Brian. Why did you have to fuck with me today? Look how beautiful it is outside. You couldn't have waited till let's say...um...never? High school wasn't enough? Huh?"

He doesn't answer. His body is too busy trembling and crying. A few punches to the face should help him answer me.

I was wrong.

He doesn't answer my questions.

I don't know what I'm doing.

I think I like it though.

After hearing a loud crack in the jaw area of his face I stop punching him. He's losing it now. He starts mumbling some weird language. I don't speak that language. I think I heard him saying mommy a couple of times. Is he calling for his mom for help? I must admit I'm surprised. His nose is swollen now and his jaw is starting to swell. He keeps mumbling for his mommy and it's starting to make me feel bad for the deed I've just done. It's just the way he is saying it. You can tell how scared he is in his voice. He is essentially an adult and still the first person he screams for is his mommy.

Wow.

I expected him to scream for the police or help. Brian probably is but his mumbling is uninterpretable. I fear someone will hear him so I put my hands over his broken mouth. I sit on him. I should have gloves on because all his blood and saliva is getting on my hands.

My heart is pounding.

My mind feels like it's racing.

Another panic attack?

No.

I like this feeling. I think I do.

I can tell he is in more pain with the force I keep applying to keep his screaming from attracting anyone. There is no need to apply all this force but who cares except Brian and who is Brian again?

Exactly.

He's nothing like I am.

I punch him a few more times.

"Brian let your friend Donovan tell you a story. A true story actually. One I hope you shall never forget."

He keeps mumbling but I don't understand mumbling. It's a language everyone speaks but no one can really understand.

"Now Brian, there once was a person I knew who came from the future. His name was Jack. He told me about a young lad like yourself who didn't know how to shut his mouth. The boy used to annoy individuals. Individuals are people Brian if you didn't know. This kid used to smoke and also talk carelessly about people's mothers. I don't know about you but he sounds a whole lot like yourself. So anyway, one day this person from the future brought a fifteen inch dildo with an eight inch circumference to this lad's house. I hope you paid attention in class to know how thick that dildo is. And you know what Jack did with that fifteen inch long and eight inch circumference dildo?"

Brian is silent.

I continue.

"Jack shoved it up the lad's ass so far and forceful that that kid who acts just like you shitted out of his mouth for the rest of his life. Brian I know you're thinking that it isn't humanly possible to shit out of your mouth. But Brian, if that kid just knew how to act and shut the fuck up, Jack from the future wouldn't have to defy the laws of where shit leaves a human's body. I love that story my friend from the future told me. At first I was like get the fuck outta here Jack. That didn't fit in his ass. Jack was like, I made it fit. How did you like the story Brian? Did you enjoy it? I hope you did. I saw Jack the other day."

I smile at him.

I like this feeling.

Brian is just lying there showing no emotions. His eyes seem like they are constantly getting wider. Brian is staring at me in a gaze. I believe Brian understands the story. Never mess with Donovan again.

My blood soaked hands leave his mouth and I check his pockets. A wad of cash was in his left one. Donovan found himself some money. Poor Brian. I leave him.

I head back to where I entered the alleyway. When I turn around to look for Brian, he is gone. I didn't even hear him run away. I didn't hear footsteps.

My job is done. My job is complete.

I never knew I had a job.

Who am I?

I'm not sure but I kinda like him.

Great job Donovan. I put the money in my pocket and walk home.

After getting home, I see my mother in the kitchen smoking weed. A joint. The smell fills up the kitchen. When did she start smoking pot?

I avoid her and go upstairs. My clothes go into the trash. When I take them off, I am amazed by how much blood I had on my clothes.

No one noticed it.

How did I not notice the blood, especially on my shirt?

Too in the moment?

Too into living?

Not really sure.

I must have been too distracted in my thoughts while my hands wiped themselves as clean as possible on my shirt. I don't remember.

I was too busy enjoying the pain I brought Brian. It really felt good hurting him. And come to think of it, nobody that saw me as I was walking home took the time to see why I had blood all over my shirt.

Their phones must have been too important.

Someone had to see me while I walked home. Cars drove by. People walked by.

I wash the rest of the blood off my hands, and take a long cold shower. In the shower it hits me what I've done. I've broken a kid's jaw and nose because he said a smart comment about my mother.

It's more than that.

What I can't get over is how great I felt hurting Brian. That look in his eyes. That helpless gaze. It was a nice view.

It was like I was in one of those horror or slasher flicks playing the killer and Brian was playing the unfortunate victim.

I didn't kill him.

I hurt him.

Brian didn't expect the unannounced meeting we had earlier. I felt good for bringing pain to Brian. I should be feeling horrible right now, but Donovan doesn't feel horrible. I should feel worthless. I should feel useless.

I wasn't useless earlier.

I'm useless now. I feel amazing but now I'm back to useless. I'm back in mother's house. Back in my room. Back to the old Donovan. Back in my prison.

Adrenaline rushed throughout my body as I was

reconstructing Brian's face. My body was on fire. Is that what violence feels like? I've never been in a fight.

I felt deranged but in control. Brian was looking at me like I was someone he had never laid eyes upon before. I look at myself in the mirror.

A new person is looking back at me.

No. It's the same old Donovan.

I miss that feeling. I have a slight smirk that I can't get rid of since I left the alley.

I look devious.

No. I look like I'm smirking.

I'm in love with this newness I'm feeling inside. Am I in love? Is this what love feels like? Am I in love with myself? I'm so lost.

Who are you Donovan?

I am not sure.

I go directly in my bed without drying off.

I use to believe that there wasn't anything else on this planet that could bring more satisfaction than a well needed masturbation session. I was proven wrong today. There are better things in life other than sitting in your room hammering your rod.

Something about bringing pain to a person that brought annoyance in my life changed that annoyance to joy.

Why is that?

I lay awake. I keep thinking about what I've done. It felt great. I got out of the house. I hurt someone and it felt good. Very good.

I'm starting to finally drift off into sleep. I don't want to dream about anything other than hurting Brian some more. That'll be a great dream. If not that then nothingness.

I want to feel that feeling again and again and again.

And again.

I felt alive.

4

A week has passed since my encounter with Brian. I haven't left the house since. I've been nothing since. I'm back to being me. Living my life in this room, in this house, in this prison. I'm free to leave whenever. I choose to stay.

I need motivation.

I enjoyed myself outside.

I should visit Brian.

I went two days before I remembered about the wad of cash I found in Brian's pocket. I had to dig in the trash for it. Good thing trash day came later in the week. Two blue rubber bands kept the money together. To my surprise it contained three hundred and fifty seven dollars.

Brian is pretty good at what he does. I don't remember the last time I had this much money. It's like he paid me to beat him up. My settlement for my pain and suffering he caused me.

I deserve more.

I'm going to visit Brian. I could use the fresh air.

He lives a few blocks up from my mother's house. I've had to walk by his house too many times because I use to miss the bus to school. It doesn't take that long to walk there. It's hot outside. There are no clouds to offer a break from the sun. A slight breeze keeps the heat bearable. When I get there, a lady is sitting outside on the porch who I suspect to be his mom.

She's old enough to be.

Sexy too.

I like sexy.

She's a thick woman. Skin appears smooth, moistened. I guess she's in her late forties. She's wearing a long tan dress that has a long V-neck which reveals a large chunk of her breasts. She doesn't have a bra on and her nipples are clearly visible.

I already like Brian's mom.

Her body still looks young from what I can see. Smooth. God has truly blessed this woman. I wonder if her butt is also blessed or she's one of those women who is blessed in the front but unfortunately not the back. I hope she doesn't lack a backside.

Brian should be worried about his mom and not about my mother. His mom has plenty to like. Plenty to crave.

Worry about your own mom.

I wave at her when she notices me nearing her porch. I'm greeted in return with a smile.

Should I talk first? I think that'll be polite. The right thing to do. I should turn around.

What am I doing here?

Just talk Donovan. Speak.

"How are you doing today ma'am?"

"You make me sound old."

"Miss?" I'm messing up already.

"Better. I'm good young man. How about you?"

"I'm alive." I feel alive. My chest is warming up. Dammit nerves. Don't fuck it up.

I'm talking to a real woman.

I'm outside my room.

I can look at breasts outside. Big breasts. Not on a computer screen.

I need to head out more.

She smiles.

"I was wondering if Brian was home."

I'm having trouble keeping eye contact with her. Her breasts are so big and her dress doesn't do the best job at concealing them.

"Yes he's upstairs. Did you hear about what happened to him?"

"No."

I want to touch her boobs.

"My little Brian got jumped by ten people last week. Three of them had guns. They broke his jaw and his nose. He had to get his jaw wired."

"That's very unfortunate."

I try not to laugh. His lies are relaxing, calming. Ten people? And they had guns? Too much pride to admit one person put him in his place.

"Yes it is unfortunate. I can't wait till I leave this place. It's a damn shame if you ask me."

"You're right. People are sick."

You're something else Donovan.

I feel new.

"Is there any way I could see him?"

"Oh sure. Let me tell him you're coming up. I don't believe you told me your name."

"Uh, Donovan. Donovan Gray, but don't tell him I'm here. You see I haven't seen him in about three years and I would like to surprise him. It's has been so long."

I lied. I'm a liar.

That's better than being nothing. It's something.

I'm making progress.

"Oh, sure. Sure. Go ahead. He should really like that."

If she only knew.

I find the steps that lead upstairs. There are photos of Brian hanging on the wall going up the stairs.

Photos of the old Brian. The Brian before my hands touched his face. It's a school photo. The one that goes on your school ID that you hate. Enough of me looking at the former Brian. Time to meet the new one.

There are five rooms upstairs. All doors are closed except one. I can see that that's the bathroom. If I was a betting man, I'd pick Brian's room to be the one with the poster that says and I quote, not making this up at all: "And I wish a nigga would, like a kitchen cabinet."

Excellent wordplay.

I knock on his door. No answer. I wait a little while then knock again. Where are you Brian? I hear someone coming to the door. The door opens and it's Brian.

I throw my hands up and shout his name excitedly. I wonder if I did look excited to see him from his point of view. I felt excited. It feels unnatural.

I'm changing.

Progress?

Progress isn't nothing.

Startled, he trips on a cord on the ground trying to run away. You forgot to close the door. Why would you run and hide in your room and not close and lock the door?

I welcomed myself in his room. His mom needs to teach him some manners. His brown eyes show fear. They're so wide and worrisome. I'm not here to hurt him. Poor Brian.

I offer a hand to help his trembling body off the floor but he doesn't accept. I pull him up gently by his shirt and point towards his bed. He sits on it.

I own Brian. I control him. I like this control.

"Hello Brian. How are you?"

No response.

"Oh that's good. Same here."

Silence.

"Why did I stop by? You know I had to check up on you."

More silence.

"You're very welcome. That's what friends are for right?"

I smile at him. He looks like he wants to cry.

I made you feel this way. I pounded your face.

His face disappoints me. It's barely bruised. Cheeks are still swollen. Nose is still crooked. I was hoping his face would be hard to look at. A face only a mother could love. It wasn't even close. I grab under his chin like my mother would to inspect the damage done.

What did I expect to see? I just hit him a few times. He has metal in his mouth.

My dreams told me he was disfigured. His face swollen purple, eyes swollen shut, and mouth busted. My dreams told me he wouldn't look like Brian any more. Sometimes he was dead in my dreams. I didn't seem to mind. He looks like the old Brian. His face just barely bruised, nose crooked, and jaw wired.

My dreams lied to me.

Stupid dreams. Can't trust my dreams now.

I lied to myself.

"Ten people did this to your face? That's terrible."

I feel his face where there are still bruises left. His grimacing tells me he's in a lot of pain. Poor Brian. "And a few had guns? Geez I wish I was there to help you bud."

"..."

"Wait what?" I bring my ear towards his metal mouth.

"..."

"I was there? I was the only one who did this to you? Nonsense. That's not what you told your mom."

"..."

"Donovan why did you have to do this to him? Now he can't even talk." I inspect his face some more. "And now he's horrified when he sees you. Poor Brian. Would you like your money back?" I wave his money in his face.

My money.

"..."

"No? But it's your money."

"..."

"You don't need it anymore? Why?"

"..."

"You stopped selling drugs? I hope so. I think that'll break your mom's heart if she knew. So where do you keep the goods?"

"…"

"Where Brian?"

He takes this brown paper bag out from under his pillow.

I take the bag.

"Is this everything?"

He shakes his head yes.

"You make me so sad. You were so talkative just a week ago. Now I can't even get a peep from you. And when were you ever going to tell me that your mom looked like that? I never told you I love women with big breasts?"

"…"

"Stay away from your mom? Silly Brian. But you talk so much about my mom. She's very pretty by the way."

He shakes his head and starts to look angry.

Yes get angry. I'm enjoying it.

"What did you just say? It's ok to talk about my mom, but not yours? That's bullshit Brian."

I'm annoying him.

He used to annoy me.

He mumbles something.

"Alright Brian. I'll let you continue doing whatever you were up to. What was that by the way?"

He gives me the middle finger.

I should break that finger.

I shouldn't. I've done enough to him.

Have you?

I've had my fun with him.

Outside Brian's mom is enjoying the weather. I let her know that it was great getting to see her son again. She was pleased. I cannot stop staring at her breasts. She must be used to it because she doesn't seem to mind so I keep at it. I just want to pull one of her boobs out and start sucking on them like they do in the millions of pornos I have seen.

Is that how it works in real life?

I'm clueless.

I'm going crazy. I shouldn't be outside. I'm not acting normal. I'm not myself. I'm too confident. I should be hiding in my room right now living the rest of the life there.

No.

As we continue to talk I get a boner. I quickly put my left hand in my pocket to grab my penis to prevent a tent from being pitched.

I should leave.

I ask for a hug.

What are you doing?

What am I doing?

She opens her arms up for a hug. I hug her making sure both of my hands get a great swipe of her breasts before they wrap around her. Her breasts felt great.

I'm going insane.

I touched breasts. I wish Brian was watching me with his mom.

I stay wrapped around her. Her breasts feel amazing against my chest. I enjoy the moment. She ask me if I'm done. Done what I wonder aloud. Hugging her. Oh. I let go making sure I get another feel. Her face tells me she noticed my hands were up to no good. My heart skips a beat. My stomach hurts.

Stupid Donovan.

I was lost in the moment. I touched breasts. They were pressed against my chest. I was lost being stupid. I got caught feeling on smooth breasts. I need a rock to hide under.

I say goodbye.

She only gives me another weird look.

I don't think I'll stop by there again. I shouldn't have left my room today. I don't know how to act in public.

I find a lighter on the ground while walking. There is no one around except two pit bulls barking and playing in a yard. I light the brown bag Brian gave me on fire. It smells like a skunk just sprayed right in front of my face. Weed has a weird smell.

I toss the bag to the dogs. I don't think they like the smell or the fire. Can't tell which one.

Dinner wasn't that good. A nasty microwave dinner. I think it had freezer burn. My mother was still at work. I have the whole house to myself. I take a quick shower and put on some fresh boxers.

I lay in bed. I feel like masturbating. That's weird. I haven't had this feeling in a while. I searched for all the porn stars I could think of that were similar to Brian's mom. It mostly consisted of women with big breasts. Simple. I masturbated to women with big breasts on a computer screen until I found something else to do that evening.

There wasn't nothing else to do.

5

Rain.

That's all the weather has been doing the last couple of days. Now, it is nowhere near as heavy as the past few days. Barely raining at that. On and off. I've been so relaxed from it. It tends to do that to people. Gives you time to think.

While I stayed in the house enjoying the relaxation the rain brought with it, I did some more thinking while watching the raindrops fall outside.

My room doesn't feel like a prison. I'm free.

I gained three hundred and fifty seven dollars from Brian. Nothing happened to me. No cops were called. I wasn't arrested. Brian couldn't even admit to anyone it was me. I enjoyed what I did to him. All I did was gain from that encounter.

Gaining is something.

I could do that to Brian a million times and the same outcome will occur. Same consequences.

Staring at the droplets falling from the sky, I ponder on what this day will bring me. I could visit Brian again. No. I need something new. I messed that up. I'm scared of his mom now. I went too far. Just go walking Donovan. I leave the house.

I'm staring at the ground as I'm walking, thinking I'll find something to do looking down there. All I manage to find is water and concrete as I go farther into town. Very few people are outside enjoying the weather. The sky is covered in clouds. I stop to observe the clouds hoping to see a vision of what my day will bring.

Just typical gray rain clouds with one that looks very much like a pair of testicles. I have such a sick mind. I watch too much porn. I could be a porn star. Make billions of dollars fucking the women I masturbate to. That won't work. My penis isn't the largest.

They like large.

The free shower has made my clothes damp, not too damp. It doesn't bother me. I haven't been paying attention while walking. I've been daydreaming about thick women with round bottoms. I check my surroundings for some.

I find none.

I just find familiar stores. Lots of them. I'm on Main Street, so I've been walking quite a while. I keep walking around town enjoying the outdoor shower until I see two very plump melons in a shirt. They belong to a white woman sitting at a bus stop with a roof over the stop across from an apartment complex. I decide to give those melons a visit.

I sit right next to her at the stop. She looks around my age. She doesn't have the prettiest face on the planet. She's wearing jean shorts with a white shirt that has flowers on it. The shorts reveal her slim thighs. An umbrella accompanies her. She is wearing a bra. A red one. Stupid bra.

The sun pierces through the clouds a little.

Her melons are a nice round shape. It could be because of that bra she has on. I'm not sure. I don't even say hi to her. I just stare at her breasts trying not to make it look obvious.

I failed.

I attempt to play it off by telling her she had a bug on her shirt and swiped at the imaginary insect on her melons, making sure I get a good feel of them tits. I'm a terrible person.

I'm aware of that.

She heard that lie a million times by the smack my face receives. They didn't even feel that nice. Great job Donovan.

Stupid bra. I turn away and stared at the wet ground. A loud horn blows. I look up for its location.

A good distance away from me I see a lady holding a turquoise purse with bright red flowing hair in the street, wearing a short yellow dress, walking with a little girl. The girl sees the van. She lets the lady's hand go and moves out of the way. A black van is inches from the lady. When the two meet, her body becomes one with the van for an instant, then violently slams onto the pavement once the van brakes, smashing her head into pavement, cracking her skull, her body rolling a few feet. Blood and the contents in her skull cover the street. Her body broken and life gone.

Blood mixes with the rain and spreads. She managed to hold onto the purse during this whole incident. The van's driver looks to see the damage done then speeds off.

The woman next to me also witnesses the whole thing. She runs away screaming into the rain. As I see her running, I see a rainbow in the sky. A young lady comes out the complex across the street trying to offer assistance to the lady even though she was already dead. You can't help the dead unless you're God lady.

Did God witness this?

Once the young lady realized that the lady lying in the street was dead, she vomits and runs off. A group of kids come running towards the scene and pulled out their phones. Pictures were taken by the children and I'm guessing uploaded to various social media networks. Multiple cars drive by. The little girl is crying. I couldn't believe my eyes. A horrible hit-and-run just happened and nobody called an ambulance or even bothered to shield the girls eyes from the nightmares that will now scar her for the rest of her life. Yet, I couldn't stop looking. I was in awe. I get up to walk towards the body. I get down on a knee when I reach the lifeless body.

Her yellow dress had blood spattered on it. The dress is up revealing the pink thong she has on under it.

Her butt cheeks are pale.

The rest of her body is also pale and badly bruised. Scrapes everywhere. I grope her two pale cheeks already knowing that nobody was around except the little girl crying in the rain. I do this until I get a boner. It takes a while. Her butt is very soft.

What the hell am I'm doing?

She's dead Donovan. It's okay. She's dead now. She's nothing. I'm just touching nothing.

I move over a little so I can see her face. She's has a very attractive face and she's wearing red lipstick. It's smeared on her face and in the street. One eye is open and the other is not. Her face is very beat up from the ground.

A good amount of the left side of her head, the side that hit the street first, is missing. That side is facing up. Some of her brain is missing and now rain occupies that area. I pour the rain out. More blood than rain leaves her skull. I search to see how her skull could have cracked open and I find out how. I see a pothole near the area of where her head hit.

That explains a lot. This town is full of them.

I turn her over so I can hold her in my arms like they do in the movies. Her breasts aren't big. I don't touch them. You can see her nipples through her dress. I can't help but smile this whole time at her dead body.

Why are you so comfortable holding her Donovan? I'm holding nothing. I'm use to nothing. It's familiar.

Hello friend.

I hold her for a while in my lap with one arm behind her back while the other is caressing her dead face while I'm smiling. She's helpless. Nobody can bring her back to life on this planet.

I think the little girl could use a huge favor God.

This lady's last experience with her daughter was very painful and for some reason I felt happy about that. I wonder what her last thought was about.

Her daughter witnessed it all. I detach the purse from

her death grip. Nothing in there was of importance to me except the six twenty dollar bills I see. I found car keys as well. Why were they not driving in the rain? I put the cash into my pocket and take out my phone to call for the ambulance. I look up for the motherless daughter. She's still crying. That makes me smile even more.

I guess I like sorrow. Oh Donovan.

The daughter is the mirror image of her mom down to the shoes on her feet except she has freckles. Elementary school must be rough for this ginger. I wipe away the tears rolling down her spotted cheeks. She's acting like her favorite Barbie was just snapped in half in front of her little eyes. She only lost a mommy. They're not all that great.

It could've been much worst. She could have died also. My smile will not go away.

I leave the mother in the street. I start a chat with the daughter.

"Hey little girl."

She keeps crying.

"Is that your mommy in the street?"

She cries harder, louder.

"You know I can use magic to bring your mommy back to life."

She looks interested but still cries.

"But, in order for it to work, you have to stop that crying. The magic doesn't work if you're crying."

You're something else Donovan and I love it.

She struggles to stop crying but submits.

"Good girl." I grin. It's crazy how powerful a lie can be. I wasn't sure that would have worked.

She attempts to smile.

"Now come with me." I take her hand. "Let's take a walk."

We walk back to Main Street. The rain continues to do its job. We take shelter in a pizza shop. There are two teenage boys working there with an older, heavyset gentleman serving as the cook. I buy her a slice and an ice cream cone with sprinkles. We are the only occupants in the shop.

During our walk, I find out her name is Sally. She's six and her favorite color is violet. Not purple, but violet she insists. I also find out that she doesn't know who her daddy is. She probably could use a dad right now.

The world we live in.

She hasn't cried since the little talk we had where her mommy died. She finishes her treat and I decide now is a great time to start my interrogation.

"Why didn't you save your mommy Sally?"

She looks confused.

"Why did you let go of her hand?"

"I don't know." Her face grows red.

"You could have saved your mommy but you didn't. You could have pulled your mommy out of the path of the van but you didn't. Why Sally? It's not nice to be selfish. Why did you allow Mommy to die?" I ask calmly.

"I'm sorry." Tears flow down her face. Her little mouth starts trembling.

Poor Sally.

"Unfortunately Sally, because of your actions, or lack thereof earlier today, my magic won't be able to bring your mommy back. But what I can do is buy you another ice cream cone with sprinkles. How does that sound?"

"But... but... Mister..." She looks so pathetic.

"Mister Purple." I fight back laughter trying to stay serious.

I'm changing. I like this change.

"Mister... Purple..."

"Mister Donovan Purple."

"Mister... Mister Donovan Purple. But you said you... you'll bring back *MOMMY!*"

"But you allowed mommy to die. You killed her, Sally and my magic won't work because of that. You can only blame yourself."

"You lied."

"That's life Sally, whether you like it or not. Now how about that ice cream cone?"

I'm smiling.

I feel alive. I'm an asshole. I like this.

She whimpers in her seat covering her face. I look away from her and notice that the two boys and cook are looking at us. They were listening the whole time. They heard my name.

I react.

I run at them and jump over the counter. I search for the biggest knife within sight and stab the closest teen to me in the head. Blood splatters in my face. Instant death.

I pick up the register and proceed to cave the other kid's head in. It takes quite a while before it caves. Felt so natural using the register. I make a mess. Stupid teen took forever to die. Blood covers my shirt. My heart is pounding. My body filled with adrenaline and the whole time I feel exhilarated.

During these two murders the cook leaves out of the back of the shop. I follow after the cook. His conditioning is lacking, and he doesn't get far. I tackle him to the ground. He hits the ground hard. He starts begging me to spare his life. I pause to think about it for a moment then begin hammer fisting the back of his head until he's unconscious. After that I reach for his forehead with both of my hands.

My heart is beating a million beats a minute. I can hear the beating in my ears.

Viciously, I jerk and pull his head back until I hear a loud crack. Struggling, I manage to lift him over my shoulder and toss him in one of the foul smelling dumpsters nearby. My back made a funny noise.

Dang.

After that I walk back to Sally. Oh Donovan. If only they minded their own business. I'm glad they didn't.

She didn't move an inch when I see her after coming through the back of the pizza shop. I make an ice cream cone overflowing with sprinkles before I hop back over the counter. She doesn't look at me when I get there. She has a blank stare that looks outside of the window at the rain whimpering. She's had herself one hell of a day. She's so confused.

I give her the ice cream, pat her head, ask where her mom's car is located and surprisingly she answers.

I leave the shop.

All I could do was bring her more sorrow by taking her with me. I think I've done plenty of that today.

My mother doesn't need another kid. I don't need one.

Poor Sally. Somebody will find her.

I remember about the register I used just recently, head back into the shop, and hop back over the counter. I slam it on the ground again and again until it bursts open. There is only a few hundred dollars inside. No more than five I suspect. I add it to the collection of money already in my pocket and hop back over.

I'm making a lot of money. Do I have a job? Is what I'm doing a job? This isn't a job. This is fun.

I like fun.

I take off my shirt, tucking it under my arm and walk home. The shirt goes in a dumpster a good distance away from the pizza shop. The rain washes all the blood from my face.

When I get to my mother's house I go to sleep without a shower or masturbation.

Oh Donovan.

I murdered three people today.

6

The world will keep spinning with or without you.

People are replaced. New families are built. Everything keeps running. Everyone will soon be forgotten. Funerals only last a day.

Next person up. Continuous turnover.

The world will keep spinning. Life goes on.

Thought of the day.

My skin is starting to darken. I spend so much time outside now. I'm rarely home.

Three people were murdered a few days ago. The three murders made the ten o'clock news but that was about it. No police chief gave an announcement saying they were in search for their murderer. No extra police cars out on patrol to search for Donovan. No mural for their deaths from their loved ones.

Sally's mom didn't even make the news.

Sad?

No.

That's life in this town. It'll eat you up then go back to what it was doing moments before.

This world doesn't have time to mourn. The world is too big to notice something so small. I'm glad I'm not as big as the world. I wouldn't get the chance to enjoy what I did. The world's blind, ignorant eyes gives me more freedom to experience this new found craze.

Can killing be a craze? I have no idea. I just enjoyed the rush it gave me. This is probably a fad.

I felt alive.

I haven't been able to sleep. I just keep thinking about what I did. It felt good. It felt right. Killing isn't right. It isn't humane. It's inhumane.

I'm an animal. I should be put down.

No.

Humans are animals. We think we're special because our brains are so evolved and advanced that we stupidly think we are better than animals. Humans are idiots. We only hide our animal side. Act like it doesn't exist.

We make laws, put on a suit and tie, build houses to live in, cut off all our natural hair and call ourselves humans.

We're animals. I'm an animal.

Murdering never appeared in my future. Never in my past thoughts growing up. I guess that's because nobody knows their true future. I never knew killing gave you such a rush. The adrenaline.

I want more. That feeling. I want to become friends with it. The control. I really ended lives.

Lives were ended because of my actions. Futures were lost. I was the reason for that. My actions made those outcomes.

The all-powerful Donovan. You're godlike.

No. I'm just doing what any feral animal does.

I'm getting cocky. Stay humble. I'm not all-powerful. I just found something that interests me. Makes my blood boil. Killing people is nothing to brag about. That's how you get caught.

I'll hate to get caught. Then my life would end. An actual prison will be my new home. I'll be a locked up animal in a cage with all the other animals in the world ready to be put down.

Be smart Donovan. You're new to all this.

I've decided to spend my day relaxing at the park. To think. My thoughts run wild because of my recent actions. Too much change too soon I believe. I like this change.

Living in my room, my prison, my coffin for the majority of my life slowly started to kill me. I decided to take control.

I decided to live. I like the control.

The weather outside is enjoyable. My body stays cooled from the wind.

I was hoping to see some fine females here at the park but there isn't any. I've been here for a couple of hours. I think I'm relaxing at the wrong park, Donovan. Enjoy the scenery. Enjoy the new you.

Is this the new me?

Walking here I had the urge again. I wanted my heart to pound, skin to ignite. I wanted that feeling again but no one around me interests me. I count fifteen adults, twenty three kids and not one of them interest me. I don't want to hurt these people.

I'm not an animal. I don't know what I am. I just know that that feeling nudges me a few times a day. I'll get over it.

Sally told me her house was near this park on Palatinate Ave. It turns out there isn't a street called Palatinate Ave. in this town. Palatinate is actually a shade of violet. The joke is on you little girl because your mommy isn't coming back.

On my way home, I see smoke coming from my street. Dark smoke. The amount of smoke in the sky tells me it isn't coming from a grill. Nothing to panic about I tell myself. Another idiot decided to catch their house on fire. I hope they have insurance.

It's my mother's house. Her car is parked in the driveway. I can't move. I'm stuck staring at the fire dance its sinister dance. The fire's intensity tells me that my mother isn't alive anymore. I can't help her. Fire has given her an end. I feel nothing. I should feel something but I believe my mind suppresses it.

Feeling.

She lived a terrible life. She worked two jobs and could barely pay her mortgage. Sometimes in the winter we went without heat. I think our water was soon to get shut off. I did nothing to help. That house was decades old. She always wanted to get it remodeled. I don't remember the last time she was happy. She doesn't get to be miserable anymore. No more stress, mother.

Where is the fire department?

Minutes go by. About ten people passed my burning former place of rest. I asked a few if they could call 911 for me. A few told me they were busy. Others asked what is wrong with the phone in my hand. I asked them if they cared and they kept coming back to the fact that I had a phone to do the calling. People in this town continue to amaze.

I call the fire department.

Firemen, cops, and an ambulance arrive to the blaze sometime after the call. I guess no one gave a shit to call because it wasn't their house. It takes some time, but the firemen manage to subdue the flames. I'm informed by one of the fireman that my mother didn't make it. I knew that already.

I wait for them to pull her body out. When they finally do I'm disappointed at my thoughts. They showed me a charred image of my mother. She isn't really burnt, cooked. Barely. Looks like the smoke took her life away.

I should feel horrible but I'm not. I guess I'm relieved. My mother doesn't have to live her terrible life and my prison is destroyed.

I'm free.

I'm going to miss my cumputer. I'll miss my mother. I'll definitely be nothing without her. Who will provide for me? The wad of cash in my pocket won't survive time. She didn't have insurance on the house. My mother couldn't afford it.

She leaves me with nothing.

Fuck.

She's really gone.

Why can't I cry?

What is wrong with me?

Depression?

The fire department ended the blaze before it burned the house to the ground. There wasn't a big crowd watching the firefighters fight the fire. I left before the officers tried to get any information from me. There was nothing for me to give to them. I have to find a new home.

Life goes on.

I'm in a hotel room outside of town. I thought about finding a park bench to sleep on but I decided to use some of my recent acquired wealth. I should have chosen a bench. This money won't last long.

It's a warm morning. I slept well. You can tell how cheap this hotel is from the piss stains on the covers. I doubt it's too expensive to buy new covers. The mattress must look horrifying. The bar of maze soap in the bathroom was already used from the previous person who occupied this room. The hotel must be having a bad year financially. This will do for now. Donovan doesn't need anything fancy.

I decide I'm going to use some of this money to open a bank account. I can't have this money on me all the time. I got nowhere to leave it now. I can't afford getting mugged. I don't trust the housekeepers here. I doubt they're paid well. I have to find a way to make more money also. I'm on my own now. No more assistance from my mother. I could also use a rush sometime soon.

Should I force myself to kill someone or just let it happen?

I'll just let it happen. Death hasn't been shy lately. Be patient.

I find a bus and take a ride on it. I take a seat all the way in the back. The purpose of this trip is to find a bank. Any commercial bank will do. I have no idea where this bus is headed but I hope it goes near a bank.

The bus isn't packed at all. It stinks like all busses do. I notice a lady with big breasts sitting towards the middle of the bus. Nobody is sitting next to her so I change my seat.

Her face is average but her breasts aren't. No cleavage is showing. I think of a plan for my hand to come in contact with her breasts. I could just ask her but that won't work.

I notice there is a newspaper on the floor near her feet. That'll work. As the bus stops at a traffic light I reach for the newspaper and purposefully fall out my seat. The fall feels fake. My acting is horrible. As I'm falling I reach for one of her breasts to grab a hold of. She is going to stomp my face in for this.

I'm unsuccessful. The momentum of the bus braking slams the right side of my face onto the steel of the seat in front of me. That's exactly what you get Donovan. She helps me up ignorant of my plan.

I feel dazed.

When I'm back in my seat I just rest my head on her tits. Fuck it. She whispers in my ear.

"I know you fell and hit your head pretty hard but I can't have you laying on me. I have a husband."

"Just give me a second. My fucking head hurts." I get more comfortable on her tits. They're comfy.

"Please get off of me sir." She's getting irritated.

"Lady I think I might have a concussion." It's not that bad.

"My breasts will not heal your *concussion!*" She pushes me off of her.

I find another seat.

I hop off the bus once it reaches a shopping center. There should be a bank here somewhere. I see a sign for one displayed outside of the grocery store. I head inside.

A white woman greets me when I reach the bank. The bank is rather small while her breasts are rather large. They catch my interest. Thank God for the lovely breasts I'm encountering today. The blue dress shirt she's wearing is revealing a ton of cleavage but hiding the good stuff. I want to meet them face to face.

She is the only one currently working. I make it known

that I want to open an account here and we make our way to her desk. Her face is mature. Late thirties is my guess. She owns short red hair. She's thick and her butt is very blessed, round, and fat for a woman her age from what I could observe from her grey suit pants as she walked to her desk.

The sight of this woman excites the guy in my pants. I need to sit down soon. This is a first. Normally women don't get me this hard unless their naked with their holes rented out behind a computer.

I should be in jail for my thoughts.

She does have all the accessories I like a women to come with during a wank session but I can't even see hers. They're hidden behind clothes. Is this love at first sight? I'm not sure but the guy in my pants thinks so.

The smile I receive from her as we sit across from each other is crooked but a cute crooked if that exists. Her bright red lipstick makes her lips so juicy. I want to kiss her. Don't get ahead of yourself Donovan. I've never been with a woman.

Nervousness is attacking me and I can't stop sweating or fucking smiling. I'm hot. She's hot, sexy. She won't stop smiling either but her job is to smile. She's paid to appear kind and friendly. I feel like I look like an idiot in front of her. This lady has put some sick spell on me.

I try to imagine her naked to relax myself. I cannot. That's a first.

I can't stop staring at her breasts. They're large. Very large.

She breaks the silence by thanking me for coming into the bank today and starts the process of getting my account set up.

"So sir would you just like to open a checking account or both a checking and savings account?" She ask as she smiles. I really like her smile. Her voice is very awkwardly proper like she's forcing herself to sound professional. She's paid to sound professional.

"What would you suggest? By the way you have a beautiful smile," I say actually forcing myself to appear mature, kind.

Her smile grows. Good compliment Donovan. I can't stop staring at her breasts. Her nipples are pressing hard against her attire. This is a tease.

"Thank you. I don't get that often. I've always thought my smile needed to go under the knife. My sister's actually did. We use to smile the same. We're twins."

A sister. Twins.

"Two beautiful smiles then." I have to find a way to touch this lady's breasts. But how? I'm too far away to try my falling trick.

"You're so sweet."

"I've been told." I'm lying. Wow Donovan. I'm having a conversation with a woman. But forget this conversation. I want her breasts.

"I suggest you open an account with both. It's typical for new account holders to open both a checking and savings account."

"Sounds great. You actually beautiful too," I say as I'm staring at her breasts.

"Am I beautiful or are my tits beautiful?" Her voice isn't professional anymore. Her real voice appears. Her smile vanished.

"Both?" My smile disappears. "Oh I'm so sorry lady but the view is worth the distraction."

Epic fail Donovan.

I should have said they're a sight to be admired. That sounds more passionate. More caring. I'm reminded I'm not good at talking to women. They don't always talk back on the computer screen.

I'm embarrassed.

If I was white, I'd actually be red right now.

"I like the honesty. How about you take me and my sister

out to dinner later. We could enjoy the company of a young gun like yourself and you can also stare at our tits all you like if you can keep a conversation. It'll be a change from all the older men who bore us. Don't bore us mister. I didn't get your name."

"Donovan. Donovan Beige." I say relaxed. She isn't mad.

"I never heard that last name before," she says curiously.

"Nobody has."

Is it really this easy? Is it really this easy to talk to a woman? Did I really just get a date?

Yes. And with two women. Twins.

I've wasted so much of my life scared to talk to a woman.

"Make sure you don't let us down Donovan. I think the offer is fair. Tits for a nice dinner and conversation."

"Will they be naked?" I had ask.

I need to find a manual on how to talk to women.

"Where do they make guys like you at? I like Donovans." Her voice returns to normal. "If only more men were open like you."

How is my head not getting ripped off by this lady? "They stopped production after me. They said Donovans can be too frank."

She bursts into laughter.

I made her laugh.

"Yeah so I currently never ever owned a car so do you or your sister mind driving?" I get a little antsy waiting to see if I ruined my chance with them.

"That's alright. How about we just relax at my place before we go out. My sister is going to love you." Her smile reappears.

Success. I have a date tonight.

"Like love love or like?" I want you lady not your sister.

"I guess you'll have to find out. I get off in an hour and we can head over then."

"Sounds great."

"We will look forward to the company," she says as she gets up to shake my hand.

"Likewise." I reply as I shake her hand from my seat.

"A little excited down there?"

"I wouldn't say a little." Dammit penis. I wanted to attempt to hug her.

"And to think Bertha said I needed surgery to attract a young man."

She walks away with a smile and newfound swagger to the front desk and I'm alone with my hard penis. Oh Donovan, you don't even know her name? She never said.

I never asked. I have to buy that manual.

The hour passes and we're off in her black sedan to enjoy an evening at the house of this lady I think I'm in love with but don't even know her name and also meeting her twin sister Bertha. I hope her sister doesn't look like a Bertha. They are twins so I doubt it.

I didn't even open that account.

I became flaccid soon after our conversation ended but it started up again as I sit in the passenger seat of the car. With every bump we hit, her breasts aggressively try to escape the prison of her shirt. She'll probably allow me to fondle them but I want to feel skin, not cotton. Meeting her today and the conversation at the bank that followed seems like the beginning plot to a cheesy porno.

I hope it ends like one. I try to start a conversation with her.

"So how big are they?" Great conversation starter Donovan.

"Oh Bertha is going to have a field day with you."

"How come?" I'm lost.

"She loves questions like that."

Still lost. "Oh okay. But do you know how big they are though?" I persist.

"Calm yourself down mister. You didn't even buy me a drink yet! You'll get all your answers when we get home."

So we sat in silence while she drove and I enjoyed the sight of her breasts. This doesn't feel right. Just feels too easy. This lady has no idea she's bringing a murderer into her home. She'll be safe. I need that body alive. I can't kill a beautiful woman.

We reach her house. She lives in a pretty nice neighborhood. The houses are not connected. Sidewalks are paved along the streets. Trees align the sidewalk. Big backyards. Swimming pools behind most houses. Multiple garages per house. White people walking their dogs. Yeah, a real nice neighborhood. I could have fun here.

We leave her car and approach her front door. I'm trying to imagine how similar their looks can be since they're twins. As long as their breasts and asses are also twins I'm in paradise. She knocks a playful tune against the door. A short time later the door opens and I'm flabbergasted that everything on this women at the door is unnaturally bigger, fuller, and rounder than her sibling counterpart while barely being concealed inside a robe.

"Hey Wendy. He's cute."

I nearly faint.

I've reached paradise.

7

"I want one! Where did you get it? I want him." Bertha eagerly asks as we sit around their living room.

It? My name is Donovan.

"He's the only one." Wendy explains as she places her hand on my thigh. If her hand would have touched my nuke I think it would have went off. It's begging to go off but war just isn't happening.

"Let me have him then. He's so cute. *Oh my!*" She places her hands on her cheeks surprised. "I just realized I only have a robe on. Why didn't you tell me you were bringing me home a treat? Now I have to get fancy Wendy," Bertha says while giving Wendy a playfully mean look.

"I like what you're wearing." I do but I don't like how she's talking about me like I'm a cute puppy Wendy just brought home.

"Oh Wendy I love him!" Bertha says ecstatically. So Wendy was right. "I could just eat you up right now. I know you want what's under this robe. But you have to pamper my feathers first honey." She says with a blowing kiss while teasing me with some extra cleavage exposure.

I must be in some dream. Did the dream start once I hit my head on the bus?

No.

I didn't hit my head hard enough. This is feeling and looking like numerous porn scenes I've seen before. Average guy finds his way into a beyond perfect woman's house for an odd reason that turns into stupid erotic conversation then sex, sex, and more sex. I hope this is real because I'll be salty if this whole thing is only a dream.

I need to pinch myself. Wake up Donovan. It's no fun if it isn't real.

"I going to change into something more proper for the occasion. I'm so excited. Come help me Wendolynn. You need to change too. You look tacky. Hurry. I can't let him keep seeing me like this. I'm not even wearing makeup. We'll be back."

Bertha hurries Wendy out of the room with her.

Such fat asses.

As the two voluptuous women go do their thing, I stay in the living room to slap myself a few times and bite my fingers to make certain this is reality.

It is.

You hit the jackpot Donovan.

You'll never be able to tell if Wendy or Bertha were twins unless you saw the images along the walls. I'm not even one hundred percent positive if that's Bertha next to Wendy in these pictures. Wendy didn't do justice when she said Bertha's lips went under the knife. Everything on Bertha went under the knife. My guess is she walked in the doctor's office and asked for everything on the menu while emphasizing to go overboard on every single procedure in the process.

This lady didn't know when to stop. I doubt she's finished. She's an addict from what I've seen in the difference in pictures. Bertha is essentially Wendy but filled with seventy pounds of silicone from unlimited procedures. But for some reason I like her unrealistic physique. It's exotic. I'm running out of room in my pants admiring the fakeness that is now Bertha. I don't know how to describe it. Everything about her image is just abnormally alluring. Silicone is literally making my dick get harder and harder.

I continue to observe my surroundings. There is nothing special about this living room. Has everything mine had but with a more expensive price tag. It's three times the size of mine too. From the pictures it's only the two of them living in this house. No husbands or children accompany them in the photos. Why live in such a large house then? Where do they get the money to live in such a place?

What's taking them so long?

Why do you even care Donovan? How am I going to get these sisters naked is what I should be worried about.

There are no new pictures of Bertha on the wall. Just the old ones where you can barely tell the difference between the two sisters.

I decide to explore the miniature castle. Large and expensive is the best description for this place. I decide to sit back in the living room. I don't want to break anything and ruin my chances tonight.

I fiddle with my fingers and wait. Be patient Donovan. Sex is on the menu tonight. Relax and wait.

I hear them in another room. They must be done changing. It has been a while. I can't wait to see them

I find them. I'm attacked with two pair of eyes. "What do you think you're doing?" They ask simultaneously.

"Just wanted to see two beautiful women."

"Are we taking too long Brown Bear?" Bertha ask.

"No. You're just so sexy."

"Oh Brown Bear. Isn't Brown Bear so cute Wendy? I think I'm in love."

"I told you she'll love you Donovan."

Brown Bear? Why is she calling me that?

"I can't wait to touch you Bertha."

"My feathers are getting pampered but not that pampered Brown Bear. What's your last name?"

"Donovan Brown."

"*Donovan Brown Bear!* I love that Brown Bear can play along. We're going to have fun tonight Brown Bear."

They're still wearing what they were wearing earlier. What were they doing this whole time?

My conversation with Bertha has become sexual. That's what I make of it. I hope somehow I can make today end with sex. I never had sex before. I've only ever had sex with my hand.

I'm not really liking how she is calling me Brown Bear though. What the fuck is a Brown Bear? I'm not a teddy bear lady.

I'm a man. She makes me sound like a child.

"Can't wait to see what Momma Bear has planned."

"That's incest Brown Bear. You're making me dry Brown Bear. Keep me wet Brown Bear. I like being wet. I'm Bertha not your Momma Bear honey."

Don't fuck this up Donovan.

"Sorry. Ummm...I'll keep you wet all night if you let me see the goods."

I wink.

I sound so corny. You're messing up Donovan. I feel corny.

I have no idea what I'm doing.

"That's what I want to hear Brown Bear. Let's go Wendolynn."

Bertha leaves for another room, motioning Wendy to follow.

"She's only calls me by my real name when she gets bossy. I think I lost out on you Donovan. I won't be able to save you tonight Donovan. Your her property now."

Their choice of words is starting to make me uneasy. I start to panic a little. "What's going to happen tonight? I don't want to be her property. I don't think I'll be into that."

"Don't look at yourself as her property. Try to see yourself as her pet."

What the fuck Wendy? "Pet? That's worse. A pet cannot be sexual with their owner. What the hell is going on?"

"Feisty. Now you're pampering some of my feathers. I'm just tickling your balls Donovan about you being her pet. When Bertha wants something she gets it as you can see Donovan. She wants you so now you're hers. Just try to stay in one piece."

Bertha yells at Wendy to stop making her wait. She needs help picking something out.

What is up with their choice of words?

I leave the room soon after. I journey around the castle looking for something to give me a better feel of these sister but I find nothing. Their choice of words had me searching for handcuffs, chains, rope, and ball gags.

I wonder how I look in their eyes.

The sexual excitement in my pants and the feeling of maliciousness is starting to overcome me.

A release is needed.

I'm also hungry. I'm starting to hunger for too many things.

I head into the kitchen and inspect the contents of the fridge. I haven't ate all day. Unfortunately there was nothing that excites my stomach except a turkey sandwich. I consume it in a matter of seconds. It was good except it had lettuce on it.

I search for that laptop I noticed earlier in one of the rooms. A wank session is well overdue.

Stop it Donovan.

These ladies are taking forever. I haven't even seen a nipple. I find the laptop and then open it. My finger presses against the power button. The laptop becomes alive. It starts up. It asks for a password. Password? I think my nuts are going to burst from neglect and this laptop needs a password.

Fine. No porn tonight Donovan. I don't need that. I need the real thing.

I think of a plan.

I start walking towards the room that Bertha and Wendy are becoming fancy in. My plan is to resort to being a peeping Tom. It was the best plan I could come up with in fifteen seconds. However as I'm getting closer to the door that's a quarter of the way open, I instantly become frozen by the sound of Bertha's voice.

"Brown Bear are you trying to get a peek? I don't like when Brown Bear peeks."

"But Brown Bear is horny." Don't call yourself Brown Bear.

You're Donovan.

"Is Brown Bear being impatient?"

"No." Yes.

"Don't worry Brown Bear. I'm worth the wait."

"Yeah."

I walk away.

I find myself in the living room again. Back where I started. Facing the TV I decide to turn it on to bypass some time. News stories play on the screen. I check to see if their subscribed to any adult channels.

Unfortunately they are not. These ladies get actual sex Donovan.

Go figure. Feeling defeated I search for a horror movie to watch in hopes of appealing to my other urge. Thankfully one is on. As I'm watching it I'm realizing how fake and unrealistic this movie is and the many I have seen before it. Hindsight is playing a huge role in this realization.

Death, blood, fear, is nothing like this shit I'm watching. What my eyes are being shown is not genuine. I'm actually a little disappointed in myself for wasting so much time watching this crap throughout the years. The hours I've wasted. A movie could never truly recreate fear and killing someone.

Flicking through the channels, I stumble upon a women's basketball game. My left hand finds itself inside my pants. After half a millisecond, my hand reappears. Nothing is arousing about watching women's basketball. I don't think I ever got soft that quick before.

What the fuck were you about to do Donovan? You have two women getting sexy for you.

I change the channel a few times and then just leave

it there. A pastor preaches on the screen. He's a middle age white male with a faint southern accent. A wide gold chain dangles around his neck as he preaches to his mass congregation. From what I see, this guy is doing very well in his ministries. As I'm paying attention to his sermon, he stops multiple times for offering.

"If you want peace in your life, give to God."

"If you want to be loved, give to God."

"Give to God if you want that new job. That new car."

"Salvation."

"Forgiveness."

"Power."

"Happiness."

Blah blah blah blah blah.

Throughout his sermon, he preaches about how you have to give to God in order to receive from God. In other words, give me money and I'm not going to do shit for you. I'm surprised these people keep on giving. His technique is pretty flawless. He breaks them down to tears with sins everyone has made before. More get broken down with failed dreams. Even more broken down with obvious needs everyone wants.

Then he threatens and reminds them about hell. They are devastated. Half of them become hysterical. Lost souls puzzled on how to fix their wrongs and receive their needs. Finally he uses God as their remedy which God is, but, giving money to the church won't save you. Especially this guy.

How dare he scam these people? Living a good life will save you. Having a relationship with God will save you. Working hard with save you. Not being an asshole like this guy will save you. But this guy is very persuasive. His bank account has to have some pretty pennies in it.

He makes my body temperature rise a few degrees.

Towards the end of his lies, a banner rolls across the bottom of the screen for prayer cloths blessed by the pastor for $79.99.

$79.99? The fuck is wrong with this guy?

A number follows. I grab for my phone. What happened to my cell phone?

I find the phone in the room and dial the number. A guy's voice speaks through the phone.

"Hello servant of God. How many prayer clothes would you like?" The guy asks all holy. It sounds so rehearsed.

"None. People buy these fucking things?"

"Excuse me?"

"You heard me."

"Look man I just work here." His voice changes to fit his actual self. "Do you want a prayer cloth?"

"No. People actually buy them?"

"Sadly they do. Sometimes we sell out. I guess they give people hope. He doesn't even bless these cloths."

"Unbelievable."

"I know. Have a nice day man."

"Yeah."

I hang up the phone.

"I didn't know you liked Pastor Meyers Brown Bear." Bertha says.

When did she come into the room?

"I don't." I turn towards her. "I like you though." I fake a smile.

"I'm flattered." She says while performing a seductive pose. So sexy.

In front of me is a person even farther away from her former self. Make-up has created her face into a new painting. A beautiful painting I must say.

A work of art.

Makeup is the ultimate tool for women that can create them into anything they dream of. Bertha dreamed of looking beautiful and makeup did the rest. She was already beautiful. Before the makeup and silicone.

Women can go from looking like a piece of shit to a goddess in a matter of seconds. It's witchcraft if you ask me.

Black magic.

Guys are disturbed and shocked when they wake up to an alien lying in bed with them the following morning. I remember stumbling on a page online that had porn stars without their makeup. You'll be surprised some of these women were allowed on camera. You'll be even more shocked that you played with yourself to some of these woman performing. Good thing faces aren't the reason men watch porn.

Bertha is wearing a long blue sparkling dress that reveals all of her cleavage while showcasing all the curves that she's been blessed with and bought. No bra is being worn. One isn't needed. They're basically floating under her dress. Her nipples are teasingly noticeable. This lady is too much. Red lipstick is painted on her lips, matching her hair, cut short like her sister's. Fancy blue heels hide her feet. I wonder if she's wearing a thong. Highly likely. I think that's the only underwear she'll wear with that ass she paid for.

I wish Bertha would buy herself a new name.

Wendy appears in similar attire but black. Aged natural beauty is in front of me as I look at her from top to bottom. If Wendy was Superman, Bertha would be Bizarro but a Bizarro you'll want a night in bed with.

Try to imagine that.

Confused I definitely am Donovan.

"Where are we headed ladies." I say as I admire the view in front of me.

"Nowhere." Says Wendy.

"Wait what? Why are y'all so dressed up then?" I ask puzzled.

"We're not supposed to look nice in the presence of a man Brown Bear?"

"No... I mean yes. I just didn't expect y'all two to dress up that much and then spend the rest of the night in the house."

"You call this dressing up Donovan? We're only wearing

dresses." Wendy answers while she flashes me her beautiful, soft breasts. Bertha nudges her angrily.

From what I've seen in that instance of her breasts exposed, the tightness of my pants have been well deserved these past couple of hours. Huge pink areolas surrounded her nipples. I'm in heaven.

"Well let's get this party started ladies!"

"That's what I want to hear Brown Bear." Bertha says as she eyes me down like a hawk ready to violate their prey.

Violate me Bertha.

What's taking her so long?

"But change that channel Donovan and Wendy turn some music on. That man has too much money already. Pastor Meyers has the biggest house on this street."

Bertha's last sentence plays in my head again.

Pastor Meyers has the biggest house on this street.

"Is anything going to happen between us tonight Bertha?"

"Sure Brown Bear. You have to pamper my feathers first."

I don't have time to pamper her feathers. I need to release one of these urges. I get up and head towards the door.

What are you doing Donovan?

Pastor Meyers doesn't deserve to live. He's stealing his congregation's money.

I hear the sisters speaking behind me but I cannot process their words. I'm focused now. I been yearning for some pleasure and the opportunity presents itself. The sisters have been wasting my time. I've been in that house for at least four hours waiting.

I'm impatient. I have a great opportunity tonight. I actually want to kill this man. I want him dead. My body becomes excited, hot.

I leave their house and venture for the home of Pastor Meyers. I'm an animal and I need to eat.

I just left two beautiful woman behind.

I'm going to regret this.

18

The biggest house on the block I find is a massive piece of architectural excellence. It baffles me that the sisters call these obvious mansions houses. I wonder what they consider a mansion in their world.

It is three stories from what I can see from the sidewalk. Massive windows. Long driveway. Four car garage. The lights in the house are off but I can make out a chandelier in the middle of the house with curved staircases surrounding it. It must be great to be a pastor in this day and age. There are no signs that this is even his house other than the size of the house. It is by far the biggest house on the block. It's about three times the size of the other houses on the block. I walk to the back of the mansion to see if I can find something that confirms that this is indeed Pastor Meyers's mansion.

There is a short fence surrounding a patio and pool worthy of being a part of this mansion. I hop over it and look through the sliding door into the kitchen. Nothing in sight is verifying that this is the residence of Pastor Meyers. No bibles. No crosses. There is mail inside on the table but I don't have eyes of a hawk.

I grab the handle of the sliding door. If an alarm goes off I should be able to make it back to Bertha and Wendy's place before the cops come searching. I've never broken into a house before. The things a guy like me will do to get his fix. Please be unlocked sliding door.

It isn't.

I check the first floor windows in back of the mansion and the third one I check is unlocked. No alarm goes off when I slide the window up. It takes some effort but I find my way through the window falling on the kitchen floor in the process. Still no alarm goes off. God must be his security system.

The moonlight is the only light I'm using as I tiptoe to the table. Evangelist Gregory Meyers is printed on the mail. So that's good. I'm in the right place. I wish I knew if that was a live sermon I was watching earlier or a recording.

The moonlight isn't helping me much. This place is a maze. I go from his kitchen to his living room, then to a bathroom, then to another living room area, then to a few bedrooms, a different bathroom, a very large closet, another large closet, then right back to the kitchen.

I didn't even see the curved staircase or chandelier I saw in the front of the house when I was outside. This place is a fortress.

The night clouds steal the only light I had. I try the maze again, knocking objects over I cannot see, breaking a few things in the maze. In the process it hits me that Pastor Meyers isn't home. The amount of noise that was being made by me without consequence confirmed it. About ten minutes later struggling around in the darkness, I find the garage. The garage is carless.

In the blackness I search for a place to hide. I'm feeling around looking to find a hiding spot. The garage is rather empty but I find something. From what I can feel it's a tool chest I'm hiding behind. It has wheels so I moved it from the wall to get in better position.

I wait.

I wait some more. I guess this is what killers do when they wait on their victims. They wait. The moonlight returns and I stand up to look around the garage. Just typical rich people garage stuff in the garage. Time which feels like hours goes by as I'm behind this tool chest. I start to get tired. I pinch and slap myself a few times to stay awake. I need to encounter Pastor Meyers first not the other way around.

It hits me as I'm behind the chest that I have no idea which door Pastor Meyers will use to get into his mansion. I'm taking a risk hiding in this garage. He could use the front, back or side door to enter his fortress, not even touching the garage door. I'll find a place to hide in his mansion. This tool chest wasn't even big enough to conceal me.

I hide in what I guess is the living room behind a couch. This place has many living rooms. More waiting ensues. It's like I'm still at Bertha and Wendy's home.

I left an opportunity at losing my virginity with a beautiful woman. Two if I was a gentleman and persuasive. A threesome could've happened Donovan.

A fucking threesome.

I'm such an idiot. My dick could be wet right now with real pussy juice.

If Pastor Meyers doesn't show up I'm going to have a fit.

What do I say to the sister's when I see them again? I blew them off. I didn't think this through. How am I going to get back to the hotel?

I don't make great decisions.

Hiding behind this couch it hits me that I have nothing to hit the Pastor with. Silly Donovan. I could use my hands but I'll like to use another method to knock him out. A brick or tool will be more fun. There are no guarantees that he has bricks in his garage so I head back there in search of that tool chest I was recently hiding behind.

I find it after a while and I check the drawers. The first two drawers are locked but I find success in the third drawer. Wrenches and hammers fill this drawer. I go for the largest wrench I can feel because with a hammer, I'll probably end his life with a blow. I'm trying to enjoy my time with him.

The wrench carries weight. The coolness of the wrench gives me goosebumps. Calm down Donovan. I'm only going to knock him out with it. I head back into the mansion.

Hiding behind the couch waiting for Pastor Meyers I pull my penis out. He's solid. I start to beat it to pass some time. I imagine Wendy and Bertha naked in front of me while I wait. They're lathered in oil rubbing their accessories.

The session doesn't last long. I quit mid-way. I want the real thing. My little guy does too.

I shouldn't be in this place. Oh Donovan. Nothing is going to happen tonight. I could be having sex right now. I slam my head against the wall in frustration.

I count all the way to one hundred and then back to zero. I go up to two hundred right after. I do some push-ups. I do some more push-ups. I do jumping jacks for a long while. I start to get tired. I'm going in and out of sleep so I slap myself a few hard times. I chomp on my tongue and the inside of my cheeks. I scream as loud as I can in case someone else has actually been in this house this whole time.

Nothing.

I decide to throw the wrench and go play fetch in the dark.

Fetch in the dark is turning out to be a bad idea. I'm breaking things by tossing this piece of metal around which I'm enjoying but I'm unfortunately tripping in the darkness and cutting myself up on the broken glass in the process.

I don't get how dogs like fetch. I throw you a ball or stick and then you go retrieve it and then bring it back to me so I can throw it again for you to retrieve it. What? Play me in some basketball dog. Learn how to talk or play videogames, man's best friend.

I end up tossing the wrench somewhere and I cannot find it. I search for it throughout this black room I'm in. I find myself searching for the wrench inside of one of Pastor Meyers' bathrooms.

Why would it be in here Donovan?

There are no windows in this bathroom and I stare into what I believe to be the mirror. I ask the mirror where the wrench is. The mirror ignores me so I try to piss on it. I'm not sure if I'm hitting it but a few splashes of piss hit me in the face so I finish in the toilet. I flush the toilet and jump from shock from the loudness of the flush. I kick the toilet for scaring me. Stupid toilet.

Leaving the bathroom my right foot steps into a puddle of my piss and slips right from under me. My face smacks into another puddle of my piss. Fuck you piss. I spit on the piss. Stupid piss. My clothes are ruined. I can't meet Pastor Meyers like this. I get up off the wet tile floor and search for some clean clothes with my ears steadily listening for any incoming vehicles.

I find one of the large closets again. It's filled with clothes. From how they feel, they are suits. Guess I'll be looking good tonight. I change my pants but I don't put on the suit jacket. I feel for a dress shirt and change into what I believe is one based only on the fact that it has buttons. I cannot find a belt so I use two ties that I found to make one. I use another tie to hang out of my pants like a penis. A tie doesn't go around my neck. I feel dress shoes but I decide to stay with the shoes I have on.

I feel on something that feels different than the other suits. Leather? A leather jacket I believe. I feel for insignia stitching on it. No stitching. It would have been cool if he was part of some biker crew. Pastor by day, Devil's Warriors by night or vice versa. I put the jacket on. It feels expensive. I can only imagine how stupid I look in my new outfit. So much for looking nice tonight. I dare not attempt to turn on a light for fear of a neighbor calling the cops. My outfit will work.

I feel for more things in the closet and feel on something hard. I try to move it but it's large and heavy. It's cold. I feel on it some more. I find a circle on it that turns. A dial? It's a safe Donovan. Oh Donovan. Guess I'm going to have to keep mister pastor Meyers alive so I can get the combination for it if he even decides to show up tonight. I sit beside the safe. I lay my face against it. I like the feel of the cold steel on my cheek. Relaxing there for a while it hits me that Pastor Meyers could be on vacation right now. What the fuck Donovan. Please let that not be true. Please God don't let pastor Meyers be on vacation or on some revival cruise with his congregation. I'm going to be sick if he is. Fuck.

Stay focused Donovan. Remember why you're here. Remember the feeling you'll feel ending his life. Remember how alive it makes you feel.

More waiting.

This is becoming so time consuming with no reward in sight. If only I could have stayed a little while longer with the sisters. I would have probably been rewarded for my patience. Is that how it works for guys? Patience equals sexual pleasure? I get out of the closet and lay on the bed that the moonlight reveals to me. Memory foam. Comfy.

Appreciating the softness and comfort of the bed, I fantasized about Wendy and Bertha naked once again. They are both oiled all over their bodies again in my fantasy. Wendy looks like a goddess while Bertha looks like an oiled up blow up doll. Bertha is one sexy blow up doll.

They're lying in bed feeding each other grapes. Everything in the room is white except for the grapes. They touch and fondle themselves on their most sensitive parts. They're asking me to join them.

I'm hard.

They are moaning a beautiful song. Bertha starts sucking on Wendy's full oiled breasts. They're sisters but it's my fantasy. I want them so bad. I want to join them but instead I'm humping the fucking pastor's bed. I've hit rock bottom Donovan.

Just give up. I scream into the pillow and stay there for some time. What am I doing with my life?

The night sky through the window gives me some comfort. The night clouds flow peacefully through the skies. Fuck you clouds. Stop being peaceful.

I throw the pillow at the window expecting it to shatter. You're a fucking idiot Donovan. I go retrieve the pillow. Pillow under my arm I decide to just lay on the ground with the pillow. I'm sorry pillow. You did nothing wrong. Neither did you clouds. I just thought this was going to be easy tonight.

"WHY THE FUCK ARE YOU IN MY HOUSE!"

Hairs erect over my body. I jump and stumble to my feet. Perspiration coats my body. That voice scared the shit out of me. A black silhouette of a man is over at the door.

The pastor.

"Hello Pastor Meyers." At last it's time.

"WHY THE FUCK ARE YOU IN MY HOUSE!" He says louder.

"I wanted to meet you sir. I follow your church sermons on the TV." This wasn't supposed to end up like this.

I'm starting to panic. I have no weapon.

"I'M GOING TO FUCKING KILL YOU."

"Stop yelling. I'm right here." Calm down Donovan. You can take him.

"DON'T TELL ME WHAT THE FUCK TO DO FAGGOT!"

An object launches from his hand.

A glass beer bottle smashes into my nose and the contents inside splash onto my face. I get dazed and stumble back into the wall. My nose is throbbing. Footsteps charge toward me. I look towards the sound of footsteps and brace myself. I see the pastor trip on the edge of the bed and then struggle pathetically to get up.

He can't.

He keeps falling over. He mumbles nonsense and keeps yelling every once in a while on the floor.

He's drunk.

He was out getting drunk at some bar.

I stomp on his head until he's unconscious.

I turn most of the lights on in the house. This house is

absolutely beautiful minus the mess I've made. The walls are filled with pictures of the good pastor. They're all basically the same picture except he's wearing a different suit and with a different person. Members of his congregation? Fellow pastors? Former wives? Why the fuck do I care?

I head into the garage. It's a totally different scene with the lights on. From what's inside, he's a carpenter in his free time. A rather good one. Three large miniature mansions are on one of the tables. Everything in these mansions were crafted by the pastor. This guy is talented.

Everything in these homes look exactly like their larger counterparts. The stoves inside look like they can be opened. There must be metal coils in them for the oven racks. I crack one of the houses open to see. There is. The handle to the toilets even move too. Cute.

I refocus. I'm getting tired. I look for some rope. There's plenty. I take some and head towards the door.

As I head out I look at his gold convertible. There are dents on the front left side and paint is missing. The headlight is cracked. There isn't another car's paint smeared on the convertible so I guess he crashed into a pole or something.

I look through the driver window. The keys are still in the ignition. Beer bottles are piled on his passenger seat and the floor. His wallet is also on the passenger seat. I open the door and get smacked with the smell of vomit. I take the wallet and keys and place them in my pocket.

I check his glove compartment. A gun resides on the top of the papers. I hesitate at first then pick it up. It's definitely real. It's a revolver with a brown wooden handle. It's unloaded. That's odd. You can't fool anyone with an empty revolver. I put the revolver back.

Pastor Meyers is on the floor sleeping or unconscious. He reeks of alcohol. I think he pissed himself. I tie his legs up followed by his hands with the rope. I catch myself yawning every once in a while. I'm exhausted.

I'm tired from sneaking around and waiting in this stupid

house. I have to plan this out better next time. Hiding and hoping they'll show up isn't going to work next time. This Pastor better be worth my time and energy.

Nobody since I encountered those individuals at the pizza shop have been worth it. No one has ignited my yearning to kill for a while until I saw Pastor Meyers the scam artist on the TV screen.

I finally turn the lights on in his room. A clock reads 4:47 am. I've been in his mansion for hours. I stare at Pastor Meyers. He's a wealthy drunk. He's a sorry man that got rich scamming people with the word of God. Poor Pastor Meyers. I hope God forgives you. I'm going to have to end you in the morning.

I'll do it tonight but I'll doubt I'll enjoy it. I'm way too tired. Sleep is more on my mind now. Maybe I'll dream about how I'll end you Pastor Meyers. I'm going to make sure I enjoy every second of it. I rub his shoulder to comfort him as if he heard what was being said in this brain of mine. He doesn't. Poor guy. The Pastor is going to be so confused when he awakens if he already wasn't confused enough. I'm too tired to remove my clothing as I lay under the covers. Sleep instantly ensues after.

I am awoken by a screaming man.

"HELP! HELP! HEEEEEEEELLLLPPPPP! SOMEBODY CALL THE COPS! HELP!"

"Go back to sleep Pastor Meyers."

He sounds louder than he was earlier. He managed to roll towards a window in his room. The fact that the window is closed and he can afford to have a good amount of land surrounding his home doesn't help his course of action.

Light shines into the room. It's morning.

No neighbor will hear his yells for help. My eyes are heavy. My body doesn't wish to move. It wants sleep. I check the clock and it reads 7:32 am. What the fuck Pastor Meyers? He keeps screaming for help. I toss a pillow at his head. His face snaps towards me. He's horrified.

You can tell in the eyes I'm starting to realize. Brian had that look. The second guy I killed at the pizza shop had that look. The look of hopelessness. The look of being scared of their future or better yet not knowing their future.

Not knowing my next move.

I think that's what scares them the most. Not knowing what's going to happen and having no control over it. Or it could be knowing what's going to happen and not being able to do anything about it. The possibilities.

His face reminds me that I stomped it. Purple, blue, and red are beautiful colors on Pastor Meyers. His lip is busted. Two teeth are missing from the top of his mouth. Blood staining his white button down shirt. His blue jeans are a shade darker from piss in his man area. I did a number on him when I stomped him to sleep earlier.

He keeps yelling. If I wasn't tired I'd probably enjoy it. I'm the cause of his yelling but I'm tired.

"It's only 7:30. Go back to sleep."

He ignores me and tries to reason with me.

"Li- listen I have money. I don't want any trouble okay? Just untie me and I'll do whatever you want. Please sir. I don't want no trouble."

"What makes you think I want your money? Go back to sleep please."

"Sir please. My cleaning lady will be here at 10:30. Just untie me and we can talk this out. If I have wronged you I'm sorry. We can talk."

"I don't want to talk. I want to sleep. Go back to sleep." I roll over.

I hide my head under his many pillows. His voice still grabs my ear's attention. He knows I'm ignoring him so he's back to yelling for help. I cannot stay in here. I get out of his bed wrapped in his covers. I walk to the door but before I leave I turn back to the yelling Pastor on the ground.

"Do you want to live Pastor Meyers?"

He stops yelling. He's shaking. "Yes. I'll do whatever you want. I have money."

"What is the name of your cleaning lady?"

The question catches him off guard. It takes him a while to find the answer in his head. It was the last answer he was expecting to answer.

"Varvara. Her name is Varvara. Please. She'll be here at 10:30. Just tell me what I can do for you."

"You can go to sleep until I'm ready for you. Where can I find a pencil and paper?"

"Sir I don't know what I did but we can talk this out."

"Where can I find a pencil and paper?"

"I have a pen and notebook in the top drawer of the desk over there. Please sir. We can talk this out."

I stare at him. I should be smiling now. I should be enjoying every moment of this but my lack of sleep is ruining these precious moments.

I get the pen and notebook and leave the room. More yelling from Pastor Meyers. He's becoming less and less audible the closer I get to his front door. His yelling is proving useless. Nobody can hear him outside. Poor Pastor. I post the notebook against the door and write *I NO NEED CLEANING VARVARA TODAY.*

To be certain that she'll comprehend I draw a broom and dust pan with a circle surrounding my artwork and slash through it. I open the door to post it but I can't because I have no tape. Fuck. I need to sleep.

I walk back to Pastor Meyers' bedroom. I saw tape in the drawer where the pen and notebook was. Walking to his room, I encounter the pastor outside of his room in the hallway squirming around on the floor. He tries to talk to me but I step over him and into the room. I get the tape, leave the room, step over the Pastor, walk to the front door, open it, post the note, close the door, lock it, walk back to where I last saw the Pastor, drag him back into his room by the rope tied to his hands, close the door so he cannot leave his room, and I go find another room that contains a bed and I go to sleep.

Finally.

A horrendous scream wakes me up. I jump out of the bed in terror. What frightens me the most is that it isn't Pastor Meyers who is screaming. It the vocals of a woman.

Varvara.

I sprint to the bedroom of the Pastor. As I'm doing so, I see Varvara running out of the house.

Fuck!

I chase after her. I trip on the doormat and bust my chin on the marble steps outside.

No.

My heart starts to pound as I watch Varvara get in her gray van and drives away as I'm lying on the ground.

No!

I run back into the house. I search for the Pastor. He isn't in his room. Sirens start to make their voices heard. I head towards the garage.

I get into the Pastor's car and put the keys into the ignition. I turn the key but the car doesn't start. I try and try but the car will not start. The sirens let me know that the cops are here. I yell and jerk at the steering wheel.

I start to panic. Think Donovan, think.

I sprint to the back of the house to the sliding door. I'm greeted by a group of police officers wearing bulletproof vest and gas masks.

Oh Donovan. Why did I think that his cleaning lady could read English? Her name was Varvara, Donovan.

Varvara!

Not Kelly. Not Anne. Not Mary. Varvara you idiot.

I turn to run to the front door but the sound of the front door being kicked in by a battering ram freezes me in my tracks. Milliseconds past and I'm surrounded by member of the local police force. Assault rifles point their dangerous mouths at me.

I'm instructed with force to put my hands behind my head and get on my knees. It's all over. I waited all night for Pastor Meyers but I became greedy because I wanted to rest so I could actually enjoy every second of his demise.

Idiot.

Shaking my head in despair staring at the tiled floor a voice speaks. I look up and it's a police officer speaking to me. The voice sounds familiar.

Too familiar.

His gas mask prevents me from knowing who is behind the mask. I've never gotten into any trouble with the police before so how do I know that voice? He steps closer to me then crouches down so he's at my level. The gas mask creates a sinister breathing sound that brings goosebumps to my skin. *WHO THE HELL ARE YOU* I want to scream at him but the words won't come out. I'm just frozen as he stares into my eyes.

His eyes makes my brain go haywire. Who are you?

He starts to remove his gas mask. My heart pounds in anticipation. The face that is revealed to me is puzzling. It's Pastor Meyers, bruises and all.

Impossible. He stands up and pulls the trigger.

Bang!

I gasp in terror in a puddle of sweat out of my sleep. I check myself for bullet holes. There are none. It was just a dream.

It felt like reality.

I check the time of the wall clock in the room. 2:17 pm. That'll be enough sleep for me in this place. Fuck that. If I learned anything from that nightmare, it's that you don't take your time with your victim.

I've read and saw countless comics and films to know that. The villain waste his time soaking up the moments before the climax of the kill that he's apprehended before he can climax. The most important part of the whole ordeal never becomes truth. It stays an idea and thought in their head forever.

That will not be me. That will not be Donovan.

My stomach growls. I need to eat. This ordeal with Pastor Meyers will have to wait a little while longer. My stomach needs nourishment.

Pastor Meyers is still tied up in his room. His face is red. His voice is lost from his useless calls for help. He's still at it though. Trying to make his sounds of need reach an ear of a savior in the world. Keep the faith Pastor Meyers. You'll be saved soon.

"No one can hear you, you know."

"What did you do to Varvara?" He asks in a way that doesn't want an answer.

She understood the note on the front door. I think of an answer that will take more life out of the Pastor.

"Well… It took some time but I managed to get your buzz saw to work in the garage. You didn't hear the saw make Varvara's legs into steaks? The meat from the thighs taste the best. I'm not really a fan of the upper body. I mean the brain is delicious but the arms and stomach are too bland. The legs are unlike any steak you'll find in the most expensive restaurant in the city. The juices are addicting. The meat is so tender."

The grin carved on my face feels permanent. Yes I'm smiling. Finally.

"Dear God. Please. Just take whatever you want." His voice cries like a kid who got all their Halloween candy taken from them. I think I over did it. Oh well. He'll survive for now.

"I want you Pastor Meyers."

"No… No… *Please!* Please just take whatever you want. I have money. Sorry! I don't know what I did."

I hold back laughter. It's crazy how a lie in one's mind can be spoken as a fact into another's mind. You don't know what you don't know. I head into the kitchen.

The fridge is packed with food. My mouth starts to water. I sift through the fridge in hopes of a worthy meal to bring joy to my stomach before the entertainment later on. Two lobster tails catch my eyes. I never ate lobster before. They are still raw because they aren't red. These lobster will do. The shells on them are pre-split.

A commercial pops into my brain of lobsters being wood-fire grilled. I remember how delicious they appeared in the commercial with grill lines browned on the tails. I don't have time, knowledge, or the equipment necessary to create the masterpiece on the commercial so I just throw them in the oven on broil with some seasoning and oil. Fingers crossed.

There is a miniature fridge in the kitchen under the counter. Alcohol of different types are the only items filling this fridge. I pull out the bottle that says whiskey. I've seen a good amount of men in movies drink this brown alcohol. I've never had it before. I have had rum, vodka, gin, and tequila but never whiskey. I guess I'm in the spirit of trying new things.

I pour myself a full glass and take a huge gulp of it. I fight back my gag reflex. My face turns silly. Throat burning I feel the alcohol coat my insides. My body warms up a few degrees. That was a little adventure. I pour the rest of the glass out in the sink. I believe I've seen some orange juice in the other fridge.

Opening up the oven, the lobster has a nice broiled look to it. I find oven mitts and take it out. Sitting at the table I observe what I have prepared. My worthy meal. Lobster tail with orange juice.

Lovely.

I get up from the table and turn the radio on that is on the counter. Gospel music plays. It stays on out of respect for being in the pastor's home. It's only right. I admire the music. The melody is nice and the words being sung are coming from the heart, spirit. I'm smiling but not like I was when I last spoke to Pastor Meyers. I think I'll enjoy this meal better in his company.

I like my life now. I love the control. I feel so alive. I don't feel like nothing. I don't feel dead. I control life, the moment of death in a person's life.

I wish I left my room earlier.

I can control a person's life switch but I can only turn it off. God can switch it on and off, life and death. God can give life and end life. I can only end life.

Does that make me the devil?

Pastor Meyers has yet to lose faith. He continues to make offers for his freedom tied up on the floor. I continue to refuse with a smile. Just a sad tied up man he is.

"You know lobster tails reminds me of a shrimp on steroids. The texture is strong. Rough. It'll be nice if I had some butter." I say chewing while waving the rest of the lobster tail around to further emphasize my words.

"There is butter in the fridge. Corn on the cob goes well with lobster. There is some in the bottom drawer of the fridge."

"Thanks." I drink some of my orange juice.

"There is also some steak. It's already cooked. You just have to-"

"Stop."

"Stop what?"

"Being nice."

"Sir I just don't want any problems. I have money. I won't tell about any of this."

"I know you won't tell," I say with a menacing smile. "You won't be able to. You are going to die today pastor Meyers. Soon actually. Spend these moments praying. Reminisce on your life. Don't waste your time begging to live."

"I have money. Please sir. What do you want?" He's says as the whimpering starts again.

"Do you know why I'm here?"

He whimpers.

"I'm here because I happened to be flicking through the

channels last night and I saw you on the TV. One of your televised sermons was on. I didn't like what I saw on there."

"You are not a man of God?" He manages to say through the tears.

"I'm actually a child of God," I say laughing slightly. "Eighty dollar prayer cloths? Spending the whole sermon preaching about giving to God. Come on Pastor. Looks like the congregation is giving to you."

"Please you are very mistaken."

"I'm pretty sure your congregation paid for this mansion and that gold toy in your garage. I don't think you're in the position to be correcting me"

"Please sir. Just listen. Television revenue paid for a vast majority of this."

"Get the fuck out of here. Really?"

"Yes. You know I've been in search of an as-"

"There you go again. Stop. Here eat this last lobster tail. I didn't really like it. Too rough. Jesus shared his last meal with Judas right?" My smile is fully erect.

Words that I believe are not from this planet are uttered from pastor Meyers' mouth. Is God speaking through him? Stop it Donovan. I don't want God to kill me before I get the chance to kill the Pastor. I finish my glass of orange juice and head to the garage.

In my dream when I frantically ran into the garage I remembered seeing a red gas can. It looked as if it was glowing as I ran past it to the car. In front of my eyes in reality, a gas can is on the floor in the same spot as it was in my dream in the garage. A picture of this red gas can is in no other memory in my mind other than my earlier dream. That's definitely a sign if I ever dreamt one.

If fear could be defined from a face, then pastor Meyers' face is the definition of fear as his eyes meet what is held in my right hand. If only I had a camera. I take a few moments to cherish this view.

His life is soon to end.

I never burned anyone alive before. I'm shaking in adrenaline. Everything is new to me lately. I've done things I never imagined doing. Who would have thought that I, Donovan, bum, virgin, would be about to burn someone alive. How many people can say that they have done that in their lives? I doubt many. I'm very fortunate to find joy in things like this. I went from beating the thing between my legs to images on a computer screen to killing people. That's one hell of a three-sixty or one-eighty.

I don't know which one.

He backs away the closer I get to him. He finds himself backed into a corner in his room. He's screaming *NO* at me. He pleads for me stop and sobs more offerings to me. I can't stop Pastor Meyers. If only you knew what I've been through to get here.

As I pour the gasoline on his head, he freaks out. He squirms around. He wipes his head all over the walls and carpet trying to rid his head of gasoline. Pastor Meyers is in love with survival. I want to tell him it's no use but I'll doubt he'll listen. I think if he could rip all the skin off of his body that is stained from gasoline he would.

The rest of the gasoline is poured all over pastor Meyers. He bites at his gasoline soaked shirt in an attempt to rip it off. He's rolling all around the floor to rid as much gasoline as possible from his clothes and body. He's trying to find the strength to free himself from the rope, clenching his teeth and everything. He just won't accept his coming death.

The straining of his face doesn't give his body enough strength to escape. I applaud you Pastor Meyers. You are a fighter. You can't fight death though Pastor Meyers. You know that. You can go a thousand rounds with death, but death always finds its hand raised at the end.

The grill lighter ignites in my right hand that I found next to the grill in the garage. I walked to the doorway of Pastor Meyers's room. He doesn't even know what's about to happen next. I call out for him but receive no reply. He's busy trying to survive, rid the gasoline from his body. It's pointless.

I toss the lighter and it stays lit half way through its trajectory before hitting pastor Meyers in the arm. Like the survivor the pastor is pretending to be, he rolls over the lighter, preventing me from retrieving it. Smart man.

Thinking quickly, I remove a lampshade from one of the lamps and lay it on its side so the light bulb is touching the carpet. I turn it on and wait by the doorway again. Pastor Meyers figures out my plan and manages to smash his head against the light bulb, shattering it before it gets hot enough to set the carpet on fire. He pulls the lamp cord out of the wall socket with his teeth for good measure.

"I could stab you to death but I've done that before. Fire will be your end today. You're probably going to heaven pastor. Just experience hell for a little."

"Please stop! *Pleeeaaaassseee!*"

"I cannot."

I go search in the kitchen and find a pack of matches.

When you see someone on fire in a movie or TV show, they flail around a little. Maybe yell a few times. Move like a zombie. Die quickly. It's nothing like what is depicted poorly on TV.

Pastor Meyers is screaming while having a fucking seizure on the floor. There is nothing comparable to what I'm seeing right now. The rush my body is receiving from the sight of Pastor Meyers' actions as he's burning is overwhelming. He appears possessed. His screams are inhuman. Parts of his skin bubble and burst. Other parts roast and darken.

My smile disappears. My face turns frightened for a moment, then serious, then back to fucking frightened. My breathing becomes heavy. I think of looking away but it stays only a thought.

I did this. I guess this is what it feels like when a drug hits you too hard. This sight is too much to handle. Thoughts of my mother burning alive in her house appear in my head. I'm not enjoying this rush at all. The pain my mother went through. She was all alone burning. I can't get images of her burning out of my head. My mother acting similar to Pastor Meyers in every way as she burns. Tears start to roll down my cheeks.

NO!

Get these images out of my head brain!

I should be enjoying this moment. Then it hits me. If I never lit pastor Meyers on fire, I would never be mourning my mother's death. If that isn't bittersweet then I don't know what is. I haven't really thought of her at all since her death. The tears vanish.

Thank you pastor Meyers. I almost forgot I ever had a mother.

The fire spreads all around the room. Pastor Meyers' screaming is muted, likely from death, but the void from the sound is replaced with the screams of the smoke detectors in the house. The flames and smoke are making it hard for me to stay in the doorway. The smoke stings my eyes. From what I can barely see, Pastor Meyers is becoming extremely overcooked, more than my mother was.

This has been an unenjoyable waste of time.

I could have chosen a night with two beautiful women.

I leave the doorway and head to the back door. I thought about taking something from his house to keep for memory sake. A trophy. That's how you get caught. I don't need no trophy from this house. I have enough trophies in my head from being in this mansion for hours upon hours.

These memories will never vanish.

9

I didn't even stay to watch the mansion burn. Disappointment prevented me from staying. I know what a burning building looks like plus too much attention will be drawn from the surrounding homes.

I heard sirens and saw emergency vehicles before I was even half way back to the sister's house. Their response time was flawless. I guess the response time is indeed different for the upper class. You don't see that in the town I'm from. They should allow that fortress to burn. Lies and false promises built that home.

I wondered who called.

That whole experience at Pastor Meyers' mansion was eerily similar to my many disappointing fap sessions. Like the experience at Pastor Meyers' mansion, it lasted very long. I had plenty of opportunities to climax and enjoy the rush of the pastor burning just like I had plenty of bust-worthy porn scenes in my past to watch. And like the many fap sessions, I didn't climax at the right scene.

I got greedy.

I went to sleep to be more energized. I wanted my sperm cannon to become overloaded so I kept delaying the climax. Like both experiences, the end wasn't the ending I wanted. I wanted to wait for the perfect moment, the perfect scene. I'd burst at a porn scene that I'll usually skip over. The fire got in the way of my view. Smoke clouded my vision. Thoughts and images of my mother burning invaded my head while I watched the pastor burn. After it all I found myself reevaluating my poor life choices.

I get off about two knocks on the sister's door before I'm attacked by a hysterically crying Bertha. Before I can manage to say anything, Bertha hugs me with all her might. If I was anything less than a man I would be crushed. The feeling of her plumped up melons pressed against my body gives me an instant hard on. Oh Bertha. I'm kissed all over my face with saliva and tears being a part of the greeting. My stiff penis rubs against her.

"Brown Bear I thought you'd never come back." She says through her quivering mouth.

"I needed to take a walk."

"A walk, Brown Bear? A walk? You were gone since last night! And you changed your clothes."

"I went home." Excellent reply Donovan.

Shit! I forgot to change back into my clothes. Hopefully that evidence burned in the fire.

"Liar!" She yells.

She presses her voluptuous breasts against me even harder. Her face gets closer to mine. I smell alcohol on her breath. I really hurt this lady.

"Okay, I'm lying. I um… um..."

"You was with some other bitch Brown Bear?" She says as she ends her hug of death and her breasts become unnaturally perfectly round again.

She wipes away her tears and gives me the look of every pissed off girlfriend. "This isn't good enough for you Brown Bear?" She says while twirling around displaying her curves in the robe she wore last night before she changed. Her nipples press against the robe. They're staring at me.

I think they are angry at me too.

"No Bertha. I was just out." I manage to say before I'm interrupted.

"You want to play games Brown Bear? I'll make sure you never leave me again for some other *bitch!*" She says as she grabs my arm and forcefully pulls me into the house.

I'm dragged into her bedroom and then pushed onto her bed. I'm told not to move a fucking muscle and Bertha leaves the room. She closes the door behind her. I get comfortable on her bed. I take my shoes off. My penis is still hard. This lady is something else.

I hear her moving from room to room. Words are mumbled loudly under her breath. I grow bored and open the top drawer of the bedside table. A huge black dildo with huge black balls catch my attention. It looks like it was cut straight off one of the many male porn performers I watch destroying those poor ladies' privates online.

There are also five weirdly shaped instruments which I can only guess are vibrators. I pick the one up that looks like an alien's finger. I switch the dial on and the weird finger vibrates violently. The sound of the vibrations are loud. It drops out my hand from its strong vibrations. I pick it up quickly and turn it off. It goes back into the drawer.

The inhuman black dildo comes out of the drawer. This dildo is heavy as shit. I guess five pounds. I don't know. Bertha fucks herself with this? It smells like rubber but I wouldn't know if it smells like a vagina because this guy's nose was never near a pussy since he was born.

I'm pathetic.

If my penis was the size of a hotdog, this dildo is the size of an extremely thick and long black man's dick. Like I could fit a couple of my dicks inside of this big black dick. Do females actually enjoy this? I know my penis is of normal size from various online penis articles and discussion boards but this thing is worthy of belonging to a giant. This dildo can't even fit into my mouth.

I tried.

Seeing this dildo and imagining it inside of Bertha gives me chills. She must have a black hole between her legs. I'm probably exaggerating about the size of this dildo but this is a huge dildo. Biggest and blackest dildo I've only ever laid hands on.

I remember visiting a website a few times of a lady whose name of her site had very little to do with what happens during her fetish videos. She could fit dildos or objects or human fists of larger size than this dildo inside of her vagina or asshole. Thinking back on that I can't believe I masturbated to those videos a few nights when there wasn't any new porn videos to watch.

The holes between this lady's legs were insane. Male fist could go in and out of her holes with no struggle. She'll prolapse after a while and smile to the camera like it's normal. The sound of it was hysterical after a gallon of lube has been filled inside her pussy and asshole. The only problem I saw from her doing this for years was that a normal penis such as the one between my legs could never touch the walls of her vagina during intercourse and that her asshole was permanently six inches in diameter. The price of making money in the porn industry. Oh how the consumers' tastes have evolved.

The thought of Bertha's lady parts appearing similar makes me sad. I stare at the dildo. "You pussy and asshole destroying big piece of shit!" I say to the big black piece of plastic. "You'll never ruin another hole again!" I growl at the dildo while attempting to snap it in half.

Not only does this dildo not snap in two but it slips out of my hand and smacks me in my face. Fuck you dildo. I take it to the window. Opening the window, I toss this dreadful pleasuring black tool as far as I can. It doesn't go as far as I hoped. It's still in my view. The neighbors will surely see. I should have attached a note to it for the next person to see it with instructions to burn it because it destroys vaginas and assholes. I loves vaginas and assholes. Especially in a scenes when they're both soaked in sexual juices. Oh man. Where is a computer with internet when you need one.

Turning away from the window the door swings opens. Bertha is in the doorways. Her makeup is ruined from her tears. She sees me near the window and starts crying again.

In her right hand is a gun and in her left hand are handcuffs and rope.

Oh shit. What the fuck did I do to this lady?

"You're trying to leave me again Brown Bear?" She sobs managing to make out that sentence.

"No… No… I was just-"

"Yes you were! Now lay on the *fucking bed!*" She demands, waving the gun in my direction.

I do exactly as I'm told and lay on the bed. I keep my eyes focused on the gun. Her cleavage is exposed but that gun has my full attention. I never had a gun pointed at me before. My heart starts pounding. All this for walking out last night? I think of words to speak but my mind cannot process any in this situation. Of all the ways to die, it's from someone I met the day before.

"Take your clothes off if they even are your clothes."

"Why?" I wonder, wishing to know in my head.

"I said take off your fucking clothes!" She walks closer to me pointing the gun closer and closer to my head.

My mind starts racing as I rip the pastor's clothes off my body. In the process the smell of smoke alerts my senses for a moment. Would she actually pull that trigger? Can I reason with her?

Yesterday I was her prize possession and now I'm her lying, repugnant, somehow unfaithful pet. And to make this all worse my encounter with the pastor wasn't even worth it. It was a waste of my fucking time.

I'm naked laying on her bed. I'm exposed in every sense of the word. The handcuffs are thrown at my chest and I'm told to put them on. I rise up against the headboard, get one cuff locked around my left wrist before Bertha walks over, gun still pointed at my head, and finishes cuffing my hands behind my back. Tears fall on me during the moment. I think of trying to subdue her and take away the gun but I doubt I'm faster than her finger pulling that trigger. Throughout all of this I'm still hard. What the fuck is wrong with you

Donovan?

"All my life I've tried to be good enough." Bertha cries out. "Do you know how hard it is to be a twin?"

No.

I go from staring at the gun to her tear soaked face. I don't see the issue of being a twin, especially an attractive one, but I dare not answer with my opinion.

"Wendolynn was always the smart one. I was the dumb twin. Wendolynn had the personality and the goods. I just had the goods. Wendolynn graduated on time with honors. I dropped out. I was the reject in the family. The beautiful imbecile my parents called me. My parents hated me. Do you know how hard it is to be the same as someone but flawed? Look the same as someone but your insides aren't wired correctly?" Bertha ask with a look of someone who is in dire need of comfort.

Mind scrambling for an acceptable answer that won't be rewarded with a hole in my head, I say "You're not flawed at all Bertha."

"Really?" She asks.

"Yes. You're perfect."

"That's what David use to say." Bertha waves the gun around as she talks.

She paces from side to side as she speaks. I get nauseous knowing that the trigger could get pulled at any second. Her crying fades and her tone becomes serious. "He was my White Bear. I love you with all my heart Bertha. We'll be together forever he used to say. This was all for him." She takes her robe off.

Scars.

Scars from the unlimited surgeries and procedures she has had on her body. The result of trying to have perfectly rounded extra-large breasts. The consequences of trying to have the body only seen, read, and imagined in fiction. Scars from every body-enhancing surgery possible. From a distance you may not even notice them, but up close you're forced to. Scar tissue covers a fourth of her body.

The price of beauty.

I'm locked in handcuffs, not knowing my future and I just want to suck on this lady's breasts. Her nipples are thick and pink. Her areolas are large. Extra-large just like all her accessories are. Oh how I want her jumbo breasts to be in my hands right now. They need a hug. They desire comfort. A gun is pointed at my skull and I want to fuck the shit out of the person holding that gun.

The scars don't bother me. Her scarred and unscarred skin looks so smooth. Her scars shine. Her hips are perfectly thick. Her ass is magnificent. It's round and jiggles as she paces.

I'm so hard right now and I'm close to my death. Her pussy lips from what I can see as she walks are not too long and not too little. They're perfect. This is torture in itself. If her body was oiled up right now I'd die from lack of pleasuring myself to a creature so unnaturally sexy. I'd take that over a bullet any day.

"First I did it for myself." She begins. "If I can't be as smart as my twin sister, my equal, then I'll have the bigger ass, tits, and lips than her. Give an edge to myself. I'll have bigger everything. Slowly I noticed a change. Once I started enhancing my appearance, guys were giving me all the attention. I'll find myself a boyfriend but we wouldn't last. He'll say we just don't click. At first I'll brush it off but then after a dozen failed relationships in a year I had to take a look in the mirror. Maybe my lips weren't juicy enough. Maybe my stomach wasn't flat like a model's. So I did what I had to do. I killed a few of my former exes, took their money and became a better Bertha."

"It took a while. Finding places to dispose of the body, gaining access to their money. It was unfortunate at first when I'd kill one of them when they had their fill of me and they had no money in the end. But I perfected my craft. Finding out their financial situation before they dumped me. It's a risky business. It'll be dumb on my behalf to kill someone who couldn't provide for my enhancements."

The whole time she talked, I tried not to scream for help. This cannot be real. She's making this all up to scare me. She's just lonely and needs company. That's all. I'm the killer. Not her. I'm the crazy one. I should be killing her. Not the opposite.

Oh God.

"So many deaths. So many surgeries. So many failed relationships. I mean I loved them all. I envisioned a future with all of them. If only they felt the same. Oh well. You live and you learn. So I continued to perfect myself so that maybe the next one will be satisfied, feel complete with what I had to offer. But many more wasted their futures on earth wasting my time until I met David."

"David loved me. My precious White Bear. He'd say oh baby you are everything I dreamed of. We were together for months. That was rare for me. Two weeks with me was an accomplishment. Then he proposed to me. I remember like it was yesterday. I thought my search for Mister Perfect was over. Then like a month after we were married, I caught him sleeping with one of the bitches at his job. A month Brown Bear. A month! I couldn't believe it Brown Bear. I was hurt. I played dumb at first. He would come home from work at night later and later. He would say his workload was increasing. Do I look like an idiot Brown Bear?"

If I wasn't tied up with a gun to my head I'd say she looked like the sexiest blow up doll I've ever laid eyes upon. I wouldn't say that to her. I'd lie and tell her how beautiful she is and how I want to touch her everywhere and have sex with her.

Instead I say nothing and just shake my head no in fear hoping someone or thing would come in here and save me from this monster if all she says is true. If only I would've stayed here last night I maybe would've gotten some type of pleasure from her.

I'm going to die a virgin.

"Thank you Brown Bear! If only White Bear knew that. I grew tired hoping he'll stop so I surprised his mistress Hillary one night while she was sleeping. You should have seen that sleazy bitch's face when she woke up with a shotgun in her face. I gave her a second to see who was holding it before I pulled the trigger. She deserved that much. She could provide my baby White Bear with something I couldn't. I never found out what she could provide that I couldn't though. I miss that shotgun."

"After that I left and went home to White Bear. He was asleep also. I wanted him to feel the pain that he brought me. He slept with his mouth wide open. He was a loud snorer but I loved it. I loved him." Bertha starts to cry again. "Do you know what lye is Brown Bear?"

Lye? "No. I don't. A lie?"

"No Brown Bear. Drain opener."

My stomach turns. What is this lady going to do to me? I'm freaking out inside not knowing my future or her plans for me. I just stare at her.

"It's used to clear clogged drains. It's very strong and effective. But back to my story. I come back home and my White Bear is sleeping. I get the lye and I poured it down his throat. He wakes up but I get a good amount down. He struggles to get up but I jump on top of him to pin him down and with both hands and I cover his mouth. It got real messy. The memory from that night will be with me forever."

She shows me the palms of her hands.

"Surgical tools will never touch these hands."

What my eyes see validates every word she has spoken. The image gives truth to all the lives she forced an early ending for. Her palms and parts of her fingers are severely burned and a darker shade than her skin tone and scar tissue.

Bite marks are evident on her palms. Chunks of meat are missing. Her husband must have struggled a great deal to escape but she wasn't going to allow it. Not after he cheated on her. If only he knew about her former lovers. I think she is worse than I am. How could she allow her palms to be burned and bitten that badly? I guess the pain he caused her outweighed the pain her hands were feeling.

How did I not notice her disgusting hands?

I hope she cannot read minds.

My penis is still hard and she still looks sexy after everything she has told me. The only reason why I can only think I'm still hard after all that is because I have no idea what she plans on doing to me. I'm tired of not knowing.

I ask "Are you going to kill me?" My heart pounds in anticipation for an answer. "Wouldn't Wendy find out?" I add to give her something to think about. My only card I can think of playing that could get me out of this situation.

"No Brown Bear. I could never hurt you." She wipes away her tears. "I'm going to make sure that you never think of leaving me for another woman again. And Wendolynn has dirt on her hands too. Now are you going to let me tie your legs to these bed posts or am I going to have to shoot you?"

"I won't be any trouble."

I'm defeated.

"That's what I like to hear Brown Bear. And look at little Brown Bear. He must like what he sees." Bertha taps and rubs her gun against my cock and balls.

My heart finds a way to pound even harder through my chest. My breathing intensifies to a new extreme.

"He does. I want you so bad. We both do." I mumble and start to break down. I can't handle all of this. Not knowing my future, gun molesting my private area.

My head drops. I lose all strength in my neck. This lady is crazy. What is she going to do to me?

"Do you think a crying Brown Bear turns me on?"

"No." I whine through my tears.

"Then stop your crying Brown Bear. I won't enjoy this as much if you're crying." Bertha says while tying up my ankles to the bedpost across from each other, spreading my legs.

She does it effortlessly because I give her absolutely no struggle. My legs are lifeless. My body has no life left in it. The only thing on me that still has life is my penis.

"Now when you are finished crying I can start."

I shove my face into a pillow to forcefully wipe away my tears. I look up to her confused and scared.

"Oh Brown Bear. I knew you were meant for me as soon as I first seen that cute brown face and those sexy brown eyes yesterday when Wendolynn brought you home to me."

She's smiling at me with those plumped animated lips of hers. Her teeth are perfect in every way. They glow as she smiles. Her body is so amazing. Take away the scar tissue, hands, and face, and she's a ten. Her face is weird but I love it. She's still holding the gun in her hand.

"You've been a bad Brown Bear. I'll be back"

She play shoots me a couple of times, making shooting sounds with her mouth. I tense up with every gunshot sounds she makes, and then she leaves the room. Her ass is so round and big. It bounces as she leaves.

She returns quickly with a black cloth. She informs me that I'm going to be blindfolded.

"No! Please don't. Please don't cover my eyes. Please." I start to break down again.

I'm starting to act like Brian and the pastor. Oh how pathetic I feel. How pathetic and useless they must have felt.

"I won't this time because you asked nicely. But next time I can't make any guarantees. Now try to relax."

She finally puts that fucking gun down. I breathe the biggest sigh of fucking relief imaginable. I won't be shot today.

Bertha starts to rub oil all over her body. Her body glistens. I try to imagine hands other than hers doing so. She teases me by playing with her breasts. Her breasts stare right at me. Veins are visible on her breasts. If only she would oil her breasts some more. She missed some areas. I'm too scared to ask for fear that she might think that I think her breasts aren't good enough the way they are.

They're perfect.

I stay silent.

She gets on the bed and is now on her hands and knees. She crawls to my penis. She blows me a kiss and then says, "Brown Bear will love me after this. You'll never leave me Brown Bear."

She starts to kiss my cock. Damn it feels good. After a minute she opens those big, red juicy lips and suck on the head of my cock like the ladies do in the pornos.

Holy Shit!

My head has become her lollipop and she's sucking the shit outta it.

Oh my god this is the best feeling I've ever felt!

My hands never felt like this.

Handrea never felt like this.

My legs shake as she tickles and pleases my head, swirling her tongue all over the tip as she sucks. She keeps switching up from light sucking to sucking it to the point that it pops out her mouth from suck to suck.

I'm restricted. I cannot free myself to reach down and caress her large round breasts while she pleases me. I'm so uncomfortable with my hands being handcuffed behind my back as I lay on her bed.

Bertha begins to fully suck my whole dick, making sure it stays nice and wet. I notice I'm starting to breathe heavily. I stare at Bertha as she works her magic on my cock. Every once in a while she looks up and gives me this seductive look. My mouth is open in awe. Bertha's sucking techniques are making her ass dance in the air. With each suck I crave more of her mouth. I grow tired of not being able to touch her perfected curves.

"I want to touch your body so bad."

"No touching Brown Bear."

"Come on. These-" I lose my train of thought from her pleasure.

My dick is the luckiest dick in the world right now. I remember what I was going to say.

"These handcuffs are digging into my back."

"Quiet Brown Bear. I'm not going to take those handcuffs off but I can do this."

My Balls!

Bertha pops and sucks my balls in and out of her mouth as she fondles my wet cock. Why do my balls being sucked feel so weird but so good? My legs try to escape their entrapment. She goes from sucking my balls individually, giving each one their personal time with her tongue, to sucking both balls into her warm mouth, massages them sexually. She continues to stroke my cock. I feel the sexual intensity and sensitivity inside and all over my cock starts to grow stronger.

Should I warn her? Yeah Donovan. I can't afford to ruin my chances for more sexual pleasure in the future. Things like this don't come often in my world.

"I'm going to cum soon."

Bertha ignores and continues her mission to never let me leave her.

I raise my voice with my warning. "I'm going to bust soon Bertha." The feeling of sexual release increases.

Her fondling of my wet cock and sucking of my balls escalate. I'm worried I'm going to shoot my load all in her hair and back.

"I'm…" and right before I finish my sentence and start to climax, Bertha starts sucking my wet throbbing cock and rubbing my balls.

I cum all in her mouth. I moan and shake during my sexual release. Bertha smiles and hums in achievement as my body tells her how great this sexual climax feels. My orgasm ends but Bertha continues to suck. My cock becomes too sensitive.

Oh Shit Bertha.

"I'm good." I'm finished cumming.

Bertha tells me no from her ongoing cock sucking.

"Oh Shit! *Ohhh Shittt!*"

I start moaning words in different languages. I start yodeling moans as a result of how intense her lips and tongue feel all over my cock, especially the head. My legs flex up. My body shakes. And the moment when I think I'm going to pass out from the intensity of the sensitive feeling my cock is overloading with, she stops.

Thank God! That was amazing. My body goes limp.

Bertha crawls off of her bed. I watch as those perfect curves move. She has defeated me with her mouth. I can't leave this lady. Never planned to either. I just needed a rush. This sexual rush trumps the disappointment I had with the Pastor.

I can live with this. This was on a whole different level. I admire her two large assets as she looks down upon me. I want her to undo my ties and handcuffs so I can feel all over her.

"That was fucking great." I let her know in case she wasn't sure from my obvious reactions.

"And I wonder why they all left me Brown Bear. I love to please my men."

"They're idiots if you ask me."

"Don't call them idiots Brown Bear. I once loved them." Her voice goes stern.

"Sorry. I want to touch and suck on your breasts so bad." I start to grow hard again.

"Don't forget about the pussy Brown Bear."

"Yeah. That too."

"My former lovers always seemed to forget about that." Bertha picks up her gun.

"No! Shit! Please! Fuck fuck fuck fuck fuck."

"Relax Brown Bear. I have to put it away." She leaves the room naked with her gun.

This fucking woman.

When she returns, she unties the ropes around my legs and unlocks the handcuffs. I grab her and pull her closer to me. I waited too long to feel upon her beautifully curved skin. Bertha's skin is so soft. Her round breasts feel better than they look. They're like the softest, only breasts I've ever felt bare. Everywhere I feel on her body, I feel the reminders of what was necessary to enhance and perfect herself.

It doesn't bother me at all. When you have masturbated to anal fisting and anal punching videos numerous times, very few things can bother a person. I tell her to lay on her back and I lightly touch her soft skin around her pussy.

She moans softly as I start to rub on her clit then insert my right index and middle fingers into her warm pussy. Bertha's warm, tight pussy soaks my two finger as I start to finger her. Her moans grow louder in approval and I thank porn for the many hours of free tutorials.

I finger Bertha for a while, making sure to feel plenty on her thick thighs and breast with my left hand. I suck on her clit every once in a while teasing her. I admire her beautiful vagina. I thank God that that evil black dildo didn't destroy the walls of her vagina. I've seen porn where a woman's pussy is a permanently opened abyss to nothingness.

Bertha pussy becomes tighter around my fingers. Her grinding increases on my fingers. I'm told to go harder. Go harder Brown Bear. I suck and lick on her clit more aggressively. I finger her harder. A little while later, she orgasms, moaning with more experienced, feminine, and less dramatic sounds than what came out of my mouth earlier.

I crawl up to her and kiss her juicy lips, grabbing her ass and whatever else on her smooth body I can get my hands on. She proceeds to stick her tongue down my throat. I'm shocked at first and a little disgusted because a few thousand of my kids could still be living on her tongue, but my penis doesn't seem to mind so I'll allow it this time. I return the favor. I grow hornier and hornier. I grab my cock and start rubbing it against Bertha's wet, swollen clit.

"Oh Brown Bear. You sure know to treat a lady in bed." Bertha moans, rubbing her clit against my cock as much as she can.

I would like to take the time to thank porn for teaching me how to please a woman. If only she knew who my sensei was. I didn't even have sex with her yet.

I'm on a roll.

"I wanna fuck you so bad."

Bertha smacks the shit out of my face with her right hand. "Brown Bear!" She yells.

"What?" I'm confused.

"I wanna fuck you so bad?" She says in a voice attempting to sound like mine with a disappointed look.

"Yeah. Isn't that what you want?" I'm so lost.

"I'm a woman Brown Bear. You make love to a woman. You fuck whores, not women Brown Bear." I'm slapped even harder.

I grab both of her hands so she won't have the chance to slap me again. She struggles, growls a little, curses at me for not releasing her. My left cheek stings and grows hot. She gives me a pissed off look but you can also tell that she likes how I grabbed her. It's the first time she experience how strong I am. I pin her hands to the bed. I think she likes how strong I am. She must love rough fucking.

I mean sex. I apologize to her.

"I'm sorry Bertha. I meant I want to make love with you."

"I'm not in the mood any more. Get the fuck off me Donovan."

I honor her command. I fucked, messed this up. I lay on the bed next to her right side. I rest my head on the side of her breasts, rubbing them in hopes she'll change her mind. I go to massage her clit.

She foils my attempt and grabs my arm I believe even

harder than I grabbed hers, moving my arm back to my side while nudging my head away from her breasts I was using as a soft pillow.

"I don't want you near me. You can go on the couch in the living room. Or better yet, you can go fuck that bitch you went to go fuck last night Donovan."

You can go on the couch? She's calling me Donovan now. Ouch. I hate Brown Bear but Donovan feels so wrong when she says it. Lord please tell me I didn't ruin my chances for future sexual adventures with this woman.

Hello?

Anyone there?

"Bertha I'm sorry. I didn't fuck any bitch or anybody last night."

"What did you do last night then?"

I draw a blank. I can't tell her what I did even though what she does is similar in nature but very different in motive. I race around in my head trying to find an answer. Every checkpoint in my brain comes up empty. Damn Donovan.

Think.

Her face grows disappointed from a lack of an answer spoken from my mouth, Bertha hops out her bed and leaves the room. Instantly my heart begins to pound. She went to get that fucking gun! I hear her footsteps return to the room with sounds of sniffling.

I go for the opened window. I'm halfway out before I feel cold steel inserted between my ass cheeks. That fucking gun! My escape attempt ends and I slowly return my upper half into Bertha's prison with the muzzle of the gun becoming friendlier and friendlier with my asshole.

I'm told to sit down. I sit under the window. My heartbeat slowly returns to normal when I see her naked, crying, shaking, struggling to keep the gun raised in my direction. Tears roll down her skin and onto her breasts. I'm killing this lady inside not giving her an answer. I'm also getting annoyed having a gun pointed at me.

"I killed Pastor Meyers." I confess.

"What?"

"I killed the pastor."

"The pastor on the TV?"

"Yes."

"The pastor that lives down the street?"

"Yes."

"Oh Brown Bear." She wipes away her tears and brings the gun down to her side. "You don't have to lie like that. If you don't want to tell me who you were fucking or what you were doing last night, fine. I'll let it slide this time. Just don't do it again. I'm tired of searching for that special one Brown Bear."

Are you serious? I killed that motherfucker. I literally kill people Bertha. I somehow enjoy it. I don't hide behind a gun and do it like you, I wish to scream at her. I become hot with rage. I want to grab her by her short red hair and drag her to what's left of the pastor's crisp corpse.

Relax Donovan. This could be good. I don't appear as the creepy psycho type. I accept her ignorance. Brown Bear has confessed his guilt and the court of Bertha finds him not guilty. I don't know if this is nice convenience. I feel like a little kid that's actually crying wolf.

Fuck that! I'm the real monster in this house. I confess my crime again.

"I tied pastor Meyers up and lit him on fire." I make my face as serious as possible.

She starts laughing. "That's the best story you can come up with Brown Bear?"

"It's not a story Bertha. Watch the news. Read the newspaper tomorrow. It'll be in there. I'm serious. Smell my clothes. Seriously. Smell them." I get up to grab my clothes and hand them to her.

Her laughing continues. "They smell like smoke. So what. That doesn't mean anything. Brown Bear you don't have one evil bone in that body of yours. Maybe a few broken ones that like to cheat on me that needs fixing, but none that could kill a man. Trust me Brown Bear. I know the look. I had to spend many hours in front of a mirror looking into my own eyes, seeing, accepting the new woman that was now staring back at me. She was sexy. Strong. She held men accountable for committing adultery and breaking my heart. Do you know there isn't surgery for a broken heart. They have surgery for everything you can think of but not a broken heart. Can you believe that?"

"Wait so you actually took the time to schedule an appointment, sit and wait at a doctor's office for your name to be called, and then actually asked a doctor if they had broken heart surgery?"

"Yes. Multiply times."

I'm baffled by Bertha's response. Oh my God I think I got my dick sucked by the sexiest mentally retarded, insane person on planet earth. The more she talks the more her ex-boyfriend killing spree stories she supposedly engaged in becomes factual. Oh Donovan. And I feasted on her kitty cat.

"At first I didn't believe the first few doctors that told me. How could you not fix a broken heart, doctor? You're a medical expert. The heart is one of the most important parts on a person's body. They would just look at me like I'm some idiot. Laugh all you want Mister Doctor that doesn't know how to fix a broken heart. You just missed out on a few thousand dollars."

My mind grows dumber with each sentence that is spoken from her surgically enhanced mouth. She's legit feebleminded. I can't tell if she's making this up or not but she did drop out of high school. Fuck Bertha. I know she had to be imperfect somewhere.

"But then there was Richard. He was the only one who knew how to heal a broken heart. I told him all the time he should have been a doctor. He healed my broken heart with his love. How didn't those idiotic doctors know that?

Richard was so smart. My Richard Bear. You know he found the cure for cancer and aids but the government stole it from him. What's taking them so long to provide it to the public? People are dying every day Brown Bear."

This whole lecture while she's giving me nonsense I fight back the urge to give her actual facts but I fear her brain might explode from knowledge overload. "Do you know what a computer is?"

"Yes Brown Bear. Wendolynn uses one at work."

"Ummm… okay." I'm slowly losing hope that her skull contains a brain. I fear her response to this next question. "Internet?"

"Internet? Is that like a net inside of a net?"

"Stop! Stop talking! This cannot be real. None of this is real. I can't do this. I really can't." I head to the door to leave this stupid thing that calls herself Bertha.

"Gotcha Brown Bear!" She rejoices.

I turn around at the doorway. Gotcha? How?

"I'm joking. I'm not some dumb blonde Brown Bear. My hair is red, not blonde. I go on the internet all the time. Richard was the exact opposite of smart. He didn't have the cure for anything. I enjoyed killing that rotten piece of shit. I admit I did think a broken heart could be fixed with surgery for a while though. I felt so stupid when Richard told me my actual heart was broken. He used to set some of the appointments for me. Silly me. I was young then. And to think he'll end up breaking my heart. He loved to play games with my head. I thought I had a future with him. Oh well. Five gunshots evaporated his actual heart."

The last sentence brought a huge smile to her face.

This chick is beyond cold blooded. That mirror she spent hours looking into gave her some crazy epiphany justifying her actions. I make a note to myself to not cheat on Bertha.

I'm her next boyfriend.

Her next experiment.

Her next pet.

Her next victim.

"I don't ever plan on cheating on you Bertha." I inform her knowing damn well that's a lie. A potential fatal one. I can't go to my grave only having sex with my hands and just one out of the billions of women on this planet. Fuck that. That's a waste of a whole lifetime.

"Oh I know. Now let me do something about that stiff cock between your legs. It's hasn't stopped staring at me since we met Brown Bear. I think my wet pussy would like to become close friends with him."

A loss of virginity and more yodeling ensues.

10

Weeks pass with no urge to kill someone to get my fix. My adrenaline high that I've enjoyed have been replaced for the time being. I haven't missed it. Bertha induced orgasms have become my new fix. Wendy has joined in on special occasions. Special occasions in which Bertha is too drunk from red wine to care. Sometimes I think Bertha just doesn't care if I'm sexually active with her sister.

I don't care either. She knows I won't leave her for her sister.

I've finally touched their most sacred part on their bodies one night a week ago. While they both gave my cock much needed mouth pleasure sixty nine style, I touched, fondled, and licked each of their assholes. I was scared at first. I didn't know how they would react.

I evolved to require a taste to observing a female's sacred hole when I would watch a porn scene and masturbate. I'll search far and wide on the web to find a high definition video where a female performer's oiled asshole stares at me for the majority of a scene while I journey to sexual climax. Then I'll hate myself for a half hour for spending hours on a Monday night beating my dick to assholes and gaping videos.

I have a sick taste.

One night with the sisters I busted six times. My dick was so sore after the fifth cum but they insisted I continue. I was surprised my cock could still get hard. I was successful in negotiations with them that if they wanted to keep making love that I have to finally partake in anal activities with them.

They're so anal about anal. They fought against it saying their pussies will miss my penis but they caved and allowed it surprisingly. My first anal experience. It was memorable.

They used various toys to please their wet pussies while I thrusted and fucked their pretty pink assholes with my lubed up cock.

I was fucking Wendy doggy style while Bertha sucked and pleased my balls. When I told them I was about to cum they attacked. Wendy backed up against me with enough force that I fell on my back with Wendy now bouncing up and down on my cock.

Bertha was now sexually abusing my balls with her mouth. Wendy's asshole tightened around my cock. As I reached climax and released, I felt the pleasure all throughout my body. As always they kept going and the sexual induced sensations became more amazing but unbearable.

I slept the whole next day in between the two, making sure I was within arm's reach to touch whichever body part on their body I desired. I'm living the life. I'm in heaven. Wendy called off of work the next day.

When the three of us enjoy meals together, I'm the talk of their world. Oh Brown Bear this. Oh Donovan that. I'm told I've brought so much joy into their lives. I think of how I'm so lucky but I remember that any sane person wouldn't be living or having sexual relations with a mass murderer and a sister that supports her actions.

I'm also the butt of their jokes during meals. *Oh I'm Brown Bear and I burn people and their houses down for a living. Blah blah blah!* They usually erupt in laughter every night after each joke. I'm left forcing myself to smile at their weak jabs. They find it so hard to believe. A silicon filled, thirty or forty something year old lady can go around executing her ex-lovers but it's unbelievable if I kill a few people.

I'm the monster in the house.

Bertha saw the news coverage of Pastor Meyers and his mansion. She thinks I just was near the mansion when it burned. That's her explanation of how I knew and why my clothes smelled of smoke. When I question her of where I received these different clothes, she tells me that I must have went shopping with that imaginary bitch I fucked.

She's never going to forget that crime I never committed.

I'm noticing she's less angry when she brings it back up on times we disagree. She hates when I leave and go out alone. I tell her I like some fresh air every once in a while. She starts crying most times and whining about how she's not good enough for me, asking me if her body isn't perfect enough. Saying things like she can get surgery if something isn't up to Brown Bear's standard.

I reassure her everything is. She grabs large bills out of her purse and hands them to me. I accept even though she gives me money on a daily basis. What am I supposed to buy? I have everything I need already.

I saw her bank statements a few times. She has fallen in love with some wealthy individuals. This goes on for some time before I reassure her enough with my devotion of love to only her through sexual acts.

One time I had to lie to Bertha during one of our sexual exploits. We were role playing and I tied her limbs to the bed posts because she was being a "bad girl". I teased her clit with some type of vibrating wand for about fifteen minutes, stopping before she came. I told her she was to stay there and suffer for an hour while I went to watch TV in the living room before I return and allow her to reach sexual climax. I left her room and I turned the TV up very loud and left the house for a few hours.

I had to get out of the house. I don't want that house, that pleasure, that mansion, to somehow become a prison.

I left a note on the fridge informing Wendy of my plan. I told her to tell Bertha that I fell asleep on the couch and to not untie her no matter what she says. I feared if she found out I was gone, a few bullets would be waiting for me when I returned. I told Wendy to make up some excuse about not wanting to interfere with our role playing.

Wendy played along. Wendy is cool like that.

I returned to a sleeping Bertha that I awoke with sexual attention to that throbbing, swollen clit of hers.

Mission accomplished. I'll live to see another day.

The actual reason I've been going out lately is that I've been searching for this kid that has been staring at me outside of the dining room window during dinner time. I noticed him three weeks ago. At first he was staring through the window using binoculars from across the street. Then I guess he became more confident and was now coming right to the window staring at me while I ate. His face is dirty most days. He always wears a green cape. He's white. I guess he's around seven years old. I nod when I see him. He gives me mean looks in response.

I tell the sisters about him but every time they look he ducks his head. They don't believe me. They think I'm playing some type of game. Why would a grown man play a game like that?

The disrespect.

One day I look up and notice him at the window while Wendy, Bertha, and I enjoy our dinner. He's holding a cardboard sign in his hands. His hands are gloved with red gloves. A house burning is drawn with crayons on the cardboard canvas. I can't hear him but I read his lips when he says "I know what you did dummy!" He sticks his tongue out and points at me.

I throw a fork at the window and sprint to the front door. Once I get outside that little bastard is already turning the corner to his freedom. My body burns with rage. *He knows!* I growl in my head. I ignore Bertha and Wendy's demands to know what is wrong with me.

The police report came out saying that foul play and arson

was the cause of the death of the Pastor and his mansion. They still don't believe I did it. They think I witnessed who did it though. They tell me not to go to the police.

Trust me I won't.

I've been searching around the neighborhood for this kid. He's like a ghost. I only see him when he's at the window staring at me while I eat. Staring at me with that stupid green cape of his. Sometimes I wonder if I'm seeing things from paranoia. I wonder if I just want someone to know what I've done.

I don't.

I grew tired walking around the neighborhood seeing all the other kids in the neighborhood except him. I asked a few kids about the little kid in the green cape but I got the hint once every kid I talked to told me "I'm not allowed to talk to strangers."

Fuck you too kids.

So I switched up my search tactics. At first I waited right outside the sister's house waiting for him to show up but I guess he would see me before I'll see him and go home. Then after a few days I changed it up again and I'll stand right by the window inside the dining room waiting to see which direction he comes from. As soon as I seen him his eyes met mine and that little sucker ran. I now knew the general location of where he could live.

I hope I'm not going crazy. I need that kid to exist. I can't be seeing things that aren't there.

I was successful yesterday.

I was walking around the neighborhood in the area I saw him coming from. I'm bored and the only thing not keeping me from going back to the sister's house is this milf jogging around the block wearing a grey track jacket with tight athletic capris. Her breasts and ass are obviously fake but they look lovely as she jogs past me every couple of minutes.

She wearing nothing under the capris. The capris wrap

perfectly around her round ass. She smiles each time she passes me. I can see the outline of her nipples. As I look at her ass while she goes for another lap in the corner of my eyes I see that fucking kid leaving his parent's house I would assume. He sees me too, giving me the finger as he goes back into the house.

You're finished kid. I walked back home now with a huge weight lifted off of my shoulders. I finally found where that fucking kid lives.

Today I wake up and nobody is home. Bertha is always home when I wake up either sleeping or cooking me breakfast. No pleasure for me this morning.

I shower, dress, leave a note on the fridge, and leave the house. I'm beyond excited. I'm calm. I'm not going to hurt the kid. I'm just going to hurt whoever he told. I could use that rush. It has been a long while. That kid lit a fire inside of me when he showed me his art project.

That fucking kid.

When I get to his house I knock on his door. No answer. I knock harder on the door. Still nothing. I go around the house looking through each window but all I see are white blinds. Dammit. I go back to the front of the house and wait by the street, sitting on the curb. Maybe someone will come home soon.

Some time passes and a guy wearing a black leather jacket approaches me.

"Hey how's it going?" He asks.

"Good. How about you man?" I stand up to shake his hand.

"Good. Everything good?" He gives me this look like he's sizing me up.

"Yeah."

"What's your name kid?"

Kid? "Donovan. Why?" I start to size him up.

"You got a last name kid?"

"Yeah. Gold."

"Donovan Gold huh? Can I ask you why you've been going around asking kids in the neighborhood where a boy wearing a green cape is?"

Shit. "I haven't done that."

"Are you a twin Mr. Gold?"

"No. Why?"

"Because you fit the description one hundred percent of every kid that described the gentleman going around asking the kids where a little boy that wears a green cape lives." He reaches inside his jacket.

A gun? Badge? I plan my actions in response to whatever arises in his hand.

My heart pounds. I'm in broad daylight. A couple are walking their dog across the street. Two kids are playing with toys near the corner of the street. Too many witnesses. I can't make that mistake again.

Fuck.

"I'm Zachary Worthy." He hands me a card. "I'm the head of the local neighborhood watch. I'm also the head prayer leader of the neighborhood prayer group."

I didn't plan for that response.

I don't respond.

"Before I came looking for you and if my memory serves me right I checked the local online sex offender registry. I don't remember a Donovan Gold listed on there."

"I'm not no pervert mister." I become pissed.

"Then why are you looking for a kid?"

"He stole my wallet."

"Don't lie to me son. Kids don't steal in this neighborhood."

I must be the worse person on the planet at lying and telling the truth. Nobody believes anything that comes out of my mouth. And what the fuck does that mean. *Kids don't steal in this neighborhood.*

"I'm not. You see any wallet in these pockets?" I turn my pockets inside out.

"If you forgot to put your name on the registry list." He reaches for what I can tell are handcuffs.

"Sir I'm not some sick faggot that preys on little boys." My voice becomes louder. "I live like four blocks down the street." I lie. "I just want my wallet. My whole life was in there."

"No need to yell. Take it easy. I'm just doing my job son. Thought I was going to have to do a citizen's arrest. I've done it before. I'll do it again."

"Yeah. Well, I'm just a guy who needs his wallet."

"Sorry to bother you Mr. Gold. I just want to keep this neighborhood as safe as possible. You have yourself a nice day." He walks away.

I look at the information on the card. "Is the address on this card your house?" I ask loud enough for him to hear me.

"Yes it is. See anything weird or would like some prayer just stop by. I'm home most nights. Or just call one of the numbers on the card."

"Thanks." We'll meet again Mr. Worthy. He doesn't believe a word out of my mouth.

I walk back to the sister's house. I don't think anybody is going to show up today at that kid's house. I'm going to get you kid.

When I walk through the door three people are relaxing in the living room drinking, Bertha, Wendy, and an obvious large black man failing to be disguised as a woman.

"Hello everyone." I say as I head to the kitchen.

"Don't be rude." The sisters say in unison. "I want you to meet Bianca."

"Sup man." I go to give him a handshake.

"Brown Bear!" Bertha shrieks. "Bianca is a lady. Now show our friend some respect and hug her."

That's a man in sheep's clothing.

"I think a handshake is enough." I try to give him a handshake but he crosses his hands, rolling his eyes in disgust of my offer.

"I'm sorry he's acting like this Bianca. He'll loosen up tonight in the bedroom. He's actually a gentleman."

"I like a bad boy sometimes." The man in a blonde wig says failing to sound anything like a natural born woman.

What did Bertha just say? "What?"

"Are you going to be difficult today Brown Bear?"

"Donovan just give her a hug."

"No! He has a dick between his legs. It's poking through his fucking dress."

Bertha pulls an object hidden between the cleavage of her breast. "You see this gun right here Brown Bear?"

That fucking gun. "You gotta be kidding me."

Wendy also pulls a gun from between her breasts. "Give Bianca a hug Donovan. We hug in this household."

"If I hug Bianca, Bianca's dick is going to stab me."

"I'm going to fuck the shit out of you boy. A hug will be the least of your worries. You'll learn to enjoy it."

Why is this happening to me?

I think of taking my chances and running to the door but I don't want to be filled with bullet holes throughout my body. I'm beyond angry. I'm confused. Men don't turn me on. Woman imposters definitely do not. People will die if his penis touches any part of me. I start shaking with rage.

"Why are y'all doing this to me? I only want you Bertha." I struggle to say.

I want to explode.

"Take a seat Brown Bear." Bertha says while motioning with the gun a seat next to the large black man.

I take a seat and he puts his arm around me, rubbing my neck in the process. He makes a comment of how hot and smooth my skin is. *Oh Donovan* I'm going to fucking stick that hand of his in a blender and turn it into a smoothie, then make him drink it before I chop his other hand off, broil it, then serve it to him on a nice plate and make him eat it only using his mouth before I get a sledgehammer and use his body as a baseball for batting practice.

"Donovan why are you being so mean to our guest."

"I'm not."

"Yes you are Brown Bear! You're upsetting me."

"I'm not going to hug or doing anything in the bedroom with Bianca. Please. Can y'all put the guns away?"

"Kiss him Donovan."

Oh God. I'm about to be the new owner of this house. I'm going to kill these sisters if I'm forced to kiss this man, this fake woman. "Bertha please. Come on Wendy." I start breathing heavily.

"It's just a kiss handsome." His lips pucker up.

There is a small, stone elephant figure on the coffee table in front of me. Before his lips gets close to mine, his head will become mush.

"Y'all better shoot me before those lips or anything else on his body touches me because this living room is about to become a scene you only see in a horror movie."

"Gotcha Brown Bear!"

Everybody except me starts laughing hysterically.

My blood boils. This was a joke? I scream at the top of my lungs in rage. I throw that man's arm off from around me and go to the other side of the room.

"Oh my God Bertha! You better thank the Lord this was all a joke because if that man did anything to me I was going to get a hammer and turn you and your sister heads into bowls of tomato soup. And you don't want to know what I would've done to him."

I try to stop shaking.

"Relax Brown Bear. I like to play a joke every once in a while." Bertha says smiling at me struggling not to laugh as if she didn't have a gun pointed at me five seconds ago trying to get me to have sex with a man.

"I don't like your jokes." I fight the urge to begin bashing their faces in with that stone elephant. Calm down Donovan. My body is burning with desire to grab that elephant.

"Brown Bear." She makes a frowny face. "I'm sorry."

"Yeah whatever. Just be thankful nothing happened." I try to calm down. I can't stop shaking. I'm starting to feel lightheaded. "I think I need some water." My legs become weak. I become dizzy.

"Poor Brown Bear. I think we went too far"

"Donovan will be fine. Let me go get him some water." Wendy leaves the room.

I stumble trying to reach a seat. White circles blind my vision. Bertha gets up and helps me to a seat on the couch away from the man. I take really deep breaths. A glass of water is placed in my hand and I guzzle it down. They all observe me caringly with looks of a concerned mother. My dizziness, shaking, body heat, rage and breathing all return to normal. Someone starts talking.

"I think you have finally found the one for you Bertha. He's tough. Mean. Too bad he's not into a woman as extravagant as me. I could teach you a thing or two."

You're a fucking man mister. "Never will that ever come into existence."

They all erupt in laughter.

"Wendy your sister got herself a good one. We have to find ourselves a Donovan."

"Sorry but I think he's one of a kind Bianca." Wendy insists.

"Oh yes Brown Bear is." Bertha rejoices.

"I'm going to go take a nap. Y'all don't know how lucky y'all are today. Y'all really don't."

I walk into Bertha's room, lock her door, and shove her dresser in front of the door.

I don't trust these people.

11

I wake up sometime midday. Clouds prevent the sunlight from fully illuminating the room. I rub my eyes to see clearer. I'm naked. My stomach rumbles. My clothes are nowhere in sight. Bertha is lying next to me with all the covers cocooned around her.

I look toward the door and the dresser is still blocking the entrance into the room. I pull the covers low enough to rub on Bertha's nipples to wake her and to also get a feel.

"How did you get in here?" I ask.

"Hush Brown Bear." She pulls the cover back up, covering her breasts, and gets more comfortable on the bed.

"Hey Bertha." I start nudging her. "How did you get in here?"

"The window. It was unlocked."

"Oh."

I take some of the covers and get comfortable myself. I hug Bertha and wrap my legs around her thick thighs. My cock instantly hardens the second it makes contact with her soft skin. I playfully pinch, rub, and make circles around Bertha's nipples with my fingers. She moans in response, rubbing her thighs on my cock, making my cock somehow become harder and harder.

"I want you Bertha. Let's make love." I start kissing on her neck.

"Hmmm." She reaches her hand behind me and grabs one of my ass cheeks. She whispers in my ear, "You're not sore back there Brown Bear?"

"Why are you asking me that?"

"Nothing. Just a little surprised. Go back to sleep Brown Bear."

"Bertha."

My stomach starts to turn.

"I'm not the only one who came through that window Brown Bear. That's all." She says grinning.

I feel all around my ass feeling for but hoping not to find any sore spots. I check my asshole last. "What are you not telling me Bertha?" I get on top of her, pinning her down against the bed with my hands on her shoulder. I stare at her right in her eyes. "Tell me now." My voice becomes stern.

Her grin disappears. She looks scared. "You think Wendy just gave you a glass of water. Bianca is a great friend of ours. We had to."

"Had to what Bertha?" I say slowly to Bertha, applying more pressure on her shoulders, body fuming with anger at the thought of being drugged and left for that female imposter to have his way with.

"You're hurting me Brown Bear. I'm sorry." Tears roll down her eyes.

I scan the room looking for what I can use to give Bertha a mastectomy. Nothing is sharp enough in the room. I struggle to keep my hands from wrapping and locking around her neck until she's unresponsive.

"Why?"

"Because."

"Because what Bertha?" My hands advance up to her neck.

"Gotcha Brown Bear!" She tells me with a smile I want to tear from her face.

"You really want me to kill you don't you? You want me to take a pillow right now, place it over that silicon filled face of yours until you're fucking dead, and then chop your body into little Bertha steaks so I can feed you to all the dogs in the neighborhood you bitch."

I receive a slap followed by another slap. "Watch that mouth of yours Brown Bear." She grabs my cock and balls before I can stop her, squeezing them, immobilizing me.

"Okay." I'm squeal, losing all rage in this ordeal.

"Now what does Brown Bear say?" Her grip tightens.

I yell. "Sorry Bertha for cursing and everything."

"That's better Brown Bear." She releases her death grip.

I roll off the bed into the fetal position, carefully holding my balls. I whisper curses to Bertha in my head so my thoughts won't be loud enough for her to hear.

"You really think I will allow anybody other than me on this earth to have you Brown Bear? You think I'll let anyone near that pretty little brown asshole of yours?" I hear her say while moving in the bed to face me.

"I don't know Bertha." I say sarcastically. "If I'm not mistaken Wendy's mouth and pussy have been home to my dick a few times." I feel like I'm going to vomit from the pain my balls are experiencing.

I feel sick in my stomach.

"And that one day that gun of yours was making out with my asshole. You never told me his name."

She yells with laughter. "Brown Bear, you're hilarious. His name is Mr. Desert Eagle by the way. You really crack me up."

"Yeah well, whatever."

"Now get up here Brown Bear and let me give you some good loving."

"I'm not in the mood." I get up and limp to the dresser. "I'm heading out. I need some air." I start to push the dresser aside then Bertha starts speaking again.

"That not what little Brown Bear is saying. Look at him. He looks so delicious. I'll make you feel better. I'll give your balls some tender loving care with my mouth."

I submit.

God dammit Donovan.

It's pretty warm outside even with the clouds. Very

few cars drive by as I walk to that kid's house. Hopefully someone is home. Every kid I see gives me mean looks. They go to the other side of the street to play when I get too close to them as I walk to reach my destination. What did you tell these kids Mr. Worthy?

Thinking of Bertha as I walk, I become hard. Could I've actually killed her during those moments of rage and confusion? I never killed a female before. I would like to think I would've. I don't love her. I love fucking her. I love the pleasure her holes bring my penis and body. Oh Donovan.

I'm lost again.

Men from my town would have beaten Bertha close to death for those pranks. Jail would have been their new home if Bertha didn't get to them first. Growing up that happened to a few of my friends' moms for lesser crimes. Former friends of mine coming into class in the morning crying about how daddy gave mommy a black eye or daddy broke mommy's collarbone tossing her around the house after a long night of drinking.

Men are pieces of shit.

Her pranks are the farthest thing from amusing. They're life threatening. Anybody other than Bertha or Wendy who would have tried that on me, their existence would've ended soon after. Better yet before, as soon as their guard came down.

One thing this has done is nourish my desire to explore my other pleasure once more. I've been seconds from exploding, killing the ones that bring me pleasure. Great pleasure. Kill Bertha and Wendy and I'm alone, back to beating my dick again. It'll be months, years before I engage with another female again sexually. I'll be stuck in a room, beating my dick, wasting my life away with Handrea, staring at monitors. The thought of my past puts fear in my heart. Some people spend their whole lives doing that. Oh what could have been if not for a few chosen decisions.

When I think on her sick pranks, Bertha's a great actor. Her sister is too. Bertha had me believing my asshole has or was going to contain a big black dick twice in a twenty-four hour period. She gave no doubt in her words or expression that I was about to be or already fucked by a man. Dammit Bertha. Be thankful the sex is beyond amazing.

She had me about to lose my mind each time. My mind stops working especially when she points that gun at me. Why am I so fearful of her fucking gun? That terrible device everyone hides behind. It turns boys into men, females into Grim Reapers. This world would be painted in a whole different image without them.

Had I not had my fill of what this earth has to offer yet? I guess not because when she faces me I become a pathetic, fearful soul, fearing death, fearing Bertha, fearing that fucking gun. Ending lives should've removed all my emotions but all it's done is give me more.

Death you're a fucking bitch.

There is a silver sports car in the driveway. Fancy. Somebody is home. I knock on the kid's door, looking around his street in case Mr. Worthy wants to pop up to bother me again.

Nothing.

I go to knock again but I hear a whisper stopping me, coming from the side of the house. I follow the whisper. It's that fucking kid with his stupid green cape and red gloves.

The kid motions me to follow him behind the house. He gets behind the house before I can and I lose sight on him. When I get to the back, a green plastic bat smacks into my balls. I fall to my knees.

"I defeated you villain. Justice!"

"What the fuck kid." I'm reminded of the pain I've felt earlier.

"Super punch!" He punches me in my face.

"Tornado bat!" He twirls that damn bat building up speed and power to crack me upside of my head.

I manage to grab the bat before he defeats me some more. I toss the bat away. "What's wrong with you kid."

"I saw you running out from that burning house. You're bad. You killed Pastor Meyers"

I get up off of my knees. "Whatever you say kid. You tell anybody?"

"No."

I don't believe him but I'll play his game. "Good cause nobody will believe you kid. Trust me. Now what's your name so I can go tell your parents you like hitting people in the balls with a bat." I need to know if they know anything.

"People call me Epic Hero. I cannot give you my secret identity. I don't trust you."

"Kid I can go in your house and tell-"

"Epic kick!" The kid yells, kicking me square in my dick before I finish my sentence. "I don't have parents. I have a mom."

"Ouch!" I back away far enough from that little devil's dick strike range.

"Welcome to the no dad club kid. Now am I going to have to punt you to another country or are you going to let me have a little conversation?" What's with kids and hitting male genitals?

"She's busy."

"Doing what?"

"Working with a customer."

"Cool kid I'll only take a second of her time." I walk to the front of the house. I need to know if this lady knows.

"She locks the door. You won't be able to get into her room."

"I'll wait in the waiting room kid."

The front door is unlocked. It's been open this whole time. The inside of the house is dark with blue shades dimming any light that was successful going through the cracks in the blinds. The light switches switch but the light bulbs don't serve their purpose. This house is an absolute mess. Trash is scattered all over the floor.

In the living room, a half-eaten TV dinner is on the coffee table, molded by time. Drug paraphernalia is resting on the stove top, waiting for some attention. I'm in the bathroom and the toilet doesn't flush, but is filled close to the top with piss and shit. Water doesn't work, explaining why the kid's face is dirty most days. I walk into what I believe is the kid's room. It's the cleanest room I've seen by far. I sit on his bed.

All that his room contains is a bed, dresser, empty bookshelf with a few articles of clothing on top, an unplugged TV, and a green frog blanket. No posters, photos, toys, pillows, books, shoes, lamp, or bedsheets. The floor is void of trash but the carpet is stained. It's humbling if anything seeing all his possessions or lack thereof.

Groans come from the room beside his. A man and a woman speak to each other. I can't make out their conversation. I hear the bed move. The sound of a dresser opens. Soon after glass clacks from inside the room. A lady yells at someone to tie something tighter. A few bitches and motherfuckers are yelled, then not too long after silence. The kid walks into his room with his bat, holding it in one hand, tapping it in the palm of his other hand, frowning at me.

"I come in peace kid. What happened in this house?"

"You found my secret lair. I must defeat you." The kid says ignoring every word I've said.

"Kid if I give you a dollar would you pay attention to anything I say?"

"Epic Hero doesn't take money from bad guys. I don't take bribes."

"I'm not a bad guy."

"YOU KILLED PASTOR MEYERS AND BURNED HIS HOUSE DOWN!" The kid screams at the top of his lungs.

My heart drops in shock of his statement. "Jesus Christ kid. Shush!" I run over to cover his mouth to prevent the rest of his testimony to be spoken to everyone with ears to hear. He mumbles words behind my hand. I look into his eyes. "If I let you talk please don't yell." I free his mouth ready to cover it if he doesn't listen.

"Why did you do it?"

"I was trying to save him from the fire kid."

"I watched you light him on fire."

Fuck kid. Is that what you do all day? Look through people's windows. "He was a very bad man. He was a church robber."

"He was nice to me."

"Well, he's not always nice kid."

"You're my arch nemesis."

"I'm on your side kid. I'm good."

Why am I attempting to make this kid believe me?

Why should I care?

Is it because of that little feeling inside telling me how horrible my actions are? Has what he has witness tainted his mind with sick curiosity?

Is it because of the poor life this kid already has, that he's a couple years away from progressing to robbing these houses he once use to only look through.

Can I save this kid?

Why does he look through people's windows? To compare his life to others?

Searching for a new home?

Family?

New mom?

A Dad?

Do I like this kid because he actually believes and knows what I've done?

I don't know.

I'm getting lost in my thoughts again.

Stop it Donovan.

"Kid what would I have to do to make you believe I'm good?"

"A hero test."

"Ummm… okay. What's that?" I'm filled with wonder.

"Follow me."

The kid sprints off. I do my best to keep up.

We end up back in the backyard. The kid is standing next to a large tree. It's the only tree in the yard.

"Okay kid. I'm ready for the hero test or whatever."

"A hero is always ready and can do anything."

"Yeah. So."

"You have to jump out this tree."

"And that somehow makes me a hero?"

"Bad guys are afraid of heights."

"Ummm…" I hold back the adult, actual truth about bad guys. "Okay. If I jump from that branch, will that be hero enough kid?"

I point to the lowest branch suitable to hold my weight.

"That branch." The kid points to a thinner branch that's higher up by about a yard.

"And that's the only option?"

His eyebrows inform me he's serious, lips frowning like an old man's. Up the tree I go.

It takes some time but I reach the branch acceptable enough to jump into hero status. I'm crouching. This branch is around nine or ten feet from the ground. It's sturdy for its size.

"So after I jump out this tree kid, I'm a good guy like you?"

"That's only the first test."

"There's more? How many more test?"

"Two more. Jump! Show your bravery."

I jump.

OWWW!

I land hard, feet first, flat footed on the hard ground, regretting I didn't roll to lessen the impact on my legs. Excruciating pain erupts in my ankles. My shins sting. I hold in my curses. I don't show the kid any signs that every part of me below my knees are in agony.

"What's next?" I say groaning slightly. I already want this fucking shit to be over.

"One thousand pushups."

"Yeah, um sure." I get on the ground in pushup position. As fast as humanly possible I say "One, two, three, one thousand," as I do the fastest three pushups in my life.

"Wow." The kid says shocked, mouth and eyes wide open in amazement.

"Yeah kid. Wow is right."

You fooled him Donovan.

"Now come with me." The kid grabs my arm, pulling me along with him.

We're back in the kid's house. We're outside his mom's room, inches from her door.

"Okay Kid. What?"

"Find out what my mom is doing in there."

"Um… what does that have to do with becoming a hero kid?"

"Heroes are also detectives."

"You don't have to be a detective to find that out. Just open the door kid."

"It's locked."

I look down at the doorknob, studying it. "Look here kid." I say, pointing to the tiny hole directly in the middle of the doorknob. "All you need is something small enough to fit inside that hole and that door will open right up. Now go find something that'll fit kid. Like a bobby pin or something."

"What's a bobby pin?"

"Um…" How do you describe a bobby pin to a child? "It's a metal thing that is skinny and about this long." I say showing him the length with my thumb and index fingers.

"When I find it, will you open the door?" He ask with a sincere voice.

"Why?"

"Because I got in trouble last time I opened the door."

What? "I thought you said the door was always locked?"

"She forgot to lock it one time and I walked in on her."

"What happened kid?"

Giggling ensues from the kid after my question. He covers his mouth to try to stop laughing. I grow curious.

"Come on kid. What happened?"

"She was sucking on this guy's wee wee."

Now I'm covering my mouth. Holy shit kid. I wasn't expecting that response. There is nothing funny about your mom sucking dick kid.

"Do you think she does that to all the guys that go into the room with her?

"How many guys you talking about kid?"

"A lot. Like there was like five guys in there already today."

His ignorance saddens me but his age helps lessen the sadness. Kid when you grow up and find out that a wee wee is called a dick or cock by grownups and that your mom is a prostitute sucking on dicks and cocks day after day for money, while getting her mouth, pussy, and asshole of hers' fucked by dicks and cocks that you find funny, filled with gallons upon gallons of cum, laughing will be the last thing you'll be doing. Laughing won't exist in your mind when you see your mom or the thought of her pops up.

The thought of man after man leaving the locked room in front of me enters into my head. Each man leaves the room still zippering up their pants zipper while the kid's mom just counts the money left for her, mouthwash on the nightstand. Should I tell this kid that his mom is a whore for hire? I look at the kid. He's giving me a look of innocence. How have you not put two and two together kid? I swear I was like five when I learned what a prostitute was.

Thanks internet.

"What else do you want to know kid? She sucks wee wees."

"She can't do that every time." He starts laughing again.

If only you knew kid. "Go look for the bobby pin kid. I'll wait here."

"Are you going to unlock the door and find out what she does?"

"Yeah. Whatever. Just go look for a bobby pin."

He heads off to find a bobby pin. I place my ear to the door, listening for sounds of lips going to town on a dick. I hear nothing. Earlier I heard his mom and some man rattling with something. Sounded like glass. The two could be asleep. Makes sense. She sucked like a dozen dicks already today. She probably put the man to sleep and also put herself to sleep from cock sucking exhaustion. Is that possible? The life of a whore.

Time is going by slowly without a single sound from the room or from the kid searching for the bobby pin. How hard is it to find a bobby pin? My mother had like a million of them laying around the house. But my mother needed them to keep her hair professional.

I find myself lightly tapping my foot. I don't feel impatient. I just need something to do. What is taking the kid so long? About a foot from me I notice a small rat scurrying on the ground along the side of the wall. The rat stops only to sniff and eat some crumbs on the floor then goes on its way. I'm surprised the rat isn't huge from the infinite supply of food on the ground.

Sometime after, the kid returns and held in his hand is a fucking dirty needle. How are you not seeing the obvious signs of what your mom is kid?

He gives me the look of a kid waiting for satisfaction from his dad or some dog waiting for their owner to reward him with a treat for fetching a stick. You're looking at the wrong person kid. I'm Donovan. Not daddy. Not your owner. I'm not going to pat your little head and call you a good boy kid.

"Where did you find that?"

"Under the couch."

"Geez kid. Get that thing outta your hands before you catch something."

"Won't this unlock the door?"

"Yes but I'll find something else kid. Not throw that thing away."

The kid throws the needle on the ground.

"Why did you do that?"

"That's what my mom does when she's throws her trash away."

Mother of the Year we got behind this door. Can't wait to meet her.

"Stay here kid."

I'm in the kitchen. If this kitchen belonged to a restaurant then it'll be closed down, quarantined, and burned to the ground. I smell rotten food and what I can only guess is vomit. My nose wishes to kill itself. How can this lady raise her child in this type of environment? The fabric on the chairs are piss stained. The table hasn't been cleared or cleaned in nobody knows how long. Dishes fill the sink covered in an ecosystem of mold. Flies dance around the trash can with maggots crawling around past meals.

Inside the top drawer near the sink are a bunch of items that have no similarity to them. The drawer is jammed a little from how filled it is but I manage to open it. I think every home has a drawer like this located in the kitchen. I fear searching and moving things around to find something suitable to open that door, especially since the kid brought me back a fucking dirty needle. Sharp and broken items fill a quarter of this drawer. I see a thin metal rod but protecting it are a couple of rusted knives. Why would you keep rusted knives?

I carefully retrieve the metal rod from the drawer. No tetanus shot for Donovan today. The drawer is left open and I return to the kid.

As I get to the hallway leading to the kid's mom's room, I'm bumped by a man in a white dress shirt, carrying his grey suit jacket folded in his left arm, with his right arm sleeve rolled up. He's headed towards the front door. He looks dazed. The man is struggling to walk in a straight line. He walks out the front door without closing it behind him.

I hear yelling and I turn to look towards the mom's room. The kid's mom is shouting at him, saying something about not being in the house when her customers are over. During this, she constantly points at him in disgust and after their talk, she grabs the kid by his shirt and smacks him with a force that knocks him off his feet. The sound of it was deafening. I winced at the sound of the smack.

The kid somehow doesn't cry but his eyes fill with water. He slowly gets up, bracing for another smack from his mom. Another doesn't come. He says something to his mom that I cannot hear then points at me. His mom looks in my direction. When her eyes meet mine she smiles a smile showing teeth that beg for dental work, giving chills down my spine from all the cocks that were unfortunate enough to spend some time in that mouth. She starts to walk in my direction.

Fuck Donovan.

The mom is about the height of an average woman. Her hair is long, dark brown with her face filled with makeup. The makeup doesn't hide that she isn't a beautiful woman. She's far from it. I don't think she knows how to properly use makeup.

The makeup fails in hiding the many scars and sores on her face, and the fact that there isn't any meat between her cheekbones and skin. This lady walking up to me is about thirty pounds too skinny. She's wearing a skirt that is meant for a child to wear, a see through blue blouse with the breast pocket dark enough to keep her nipples concealed. She isn't wearing a bra and I doubt any type of panties are being worn. To emphasize the sight of the woman, my dick stays so soft the entire time she approaches me.

A foul odor arises as she opens her mouth to speak to me.

I hold my breath.

"You don't look like the type in need of some medication. I see you as the pleasure seeking type." The mom says as she lightly grabs my newly transformed micropenis.

"No thank you." Donovan remind yourself to burn these clothes.

She backs away a distance. "You the cops?"

Yeah I'm the cops, and you're being arrested for being a shitty mom. "No."

The mom looks me up and down. She goes to the closest window and checks outside for what I can guess are any signs of law enforcement. I never knew I looked like the law enforcement type. When my answer is confirmed she approaches me again with that sick smile of hers.

"What you into then cutie pie?"

"I'm gay." Hope my soft penis confirmed that lie.

"I gotta friend you might like."

"I only like a certain type of guy."

"I didn't even tell you what he looks like."

"I know. I'm not interested."

"Why the fuck are you inside of my house?" She yells angrily.

I back away. "Miss this is going to sound really childish but I was doing one of your son's hero test which required-"

"Don't tell her." The kid barks.

"You little shit. What did I tell you about getting in grown folks conversations. Am I gonna have to smack that stupid face of yours again?" She chargers towards her son.

I grab her by the back of her blouse, my hold jerks her body back, and I throw her to the ground. She yells profanities and other words but I ignore her as I pin her onto the ground under me. She struggles to escape but I won't allow it. The kid stays frozen in place. Afraid is the look his face is making, especially from the look of his eyes becoming unnaturally wide, watching me keep his mom grounded on the floor.

She gathers all the saliva in her mouth and spits it all

over my face. I scream for fear of catching every disease known to man, letting go of her arms to get this fucking shit off me.

I can't fucking see. This spit is all in my eyes. I'm freaking out. If there was cum in her mouth I'm going to kill this lady. There could be kids chilling, squirming around on my fucking face right now.

I'm going to kill this bitch.

Nails dig into my face. I grab her hands but pulling on them assist her in ripping more flesh from my face. I guess where her head is located and swing a fist. Nothing. I swing some more. Still nothing. Where the fuck is this lady's face at? The pain of her dirty fucking nails inside parts of my face is becoming unbearable. I'm forced to use my hands to pull her nails, finger by finger, from my face. I heard two of her fingers snap in doing so.

Fucking bitch.

I'm using my shirt to wipe this tainted mess off of my face. I can finally see again. The kid's mom is a step away from me, in her natural position, on her knees, grabbing her left hand, groaning, cursing nonsense and threats towards me.

I hope I didn't catch anything.

I'm tainted.

"My fucking hand is broken." She moans, eyes watering from the pain.

"Guess you won't be able service two clients at once until further notice you bitch." I say with my hands lightly touching the new damage to my face. Fuck this shit hurts.

"You are fucking dead asshole. I'm calling the cops." She gets up, using her good hand to help her.

"Good luck hiding all the drugs and shit you got laying around the house."

The kid's mom walks away without a reply. I turn to the kid.

"Hey kid. You okay?"

"Yes." The kid says. You can tell he isn't by his legs shaking.

"Could you get me some alcohol? I don't want these scratches on my face to get infected kid."

"You're weird." He says, giving me this confused look.

"Just get the alcohol please."

He heads off.

Seconds pass and the kid returns. In his hand is a bottle of rum, eighty proof. Jesus fucking Christ kid! "You never scraped your knee before? I'm talking about that type of alcohol kid. I'm literally becoming infected by the second kid."

"My mom just tells me to suck it up when I hurt myself."

"She would say suck it up."

"Why would she say that?"

"When you reach the age of common sense kid, you'll know. I'll let your brain wait until that day so you won't hate the world at such a young age. Enjoy seeing the world through eyes of ignorance kid. Oh how you will miss those days."

The kid stares at me, lost.

"Aren't we all kid. Did you see what your mom was doing?"

"I had to find my steel bat." She yells behind me, swinging the bat, striking my left arm as I turn towards her.

"Fuck... Shit lady!" What the fuck is with this family and bats?

"That's for my hand you dickhead."

"Now for being in my fucking house." She raises the bat.

I tackle her before she swings. She hits the ground hard, her head bouncing off the floor. She's dazed but I smack her a few times to bring her back into this world. I need her full attention. I'm more forceful this time, using as much of my weight to keep her pinned to the floor. If she spits in my face again, I'm going to head butt her to death if possible.

Shit, I'll make it possible.

"Listen here lady."

"I should have got my steak knife instead."

"You live and you learn. Now listen."

"I'm not going to listen to you, you piece of shit. Get off of me. You're hurting me." She turns her face towards her son. "Call 911 baby."

He doesn't move an inch. Good job kid.

"If you don't shut the fuck up lady, I'm going to manually disconnect your spine from your body."

Fear enters her words. "You wouldn't."

"Do you really want to know if I'm serious?"

She takes a moment, mouth trembling. "No."

"Good." I begin. "You remind me of a lady I seen before. She is what you would call an adult performer. If you're too dumb to know what an adult performer is, she is a porn star. If you still don't know what a porn star is, she is a lady that has sex for money on camera. So she's basically what you are but a little more professional if you call your line of work professional."

"You think I'm going to sit here and let you disrespect me."

"Yes. Now stop talking before I get that steak knife you spoke of and remove that tongue of yours. Kid, please get that steak knife just in case."

The kid runs off. He returns with the steak knife soon after.

"You little bitch. I should have never kept you."

I take the knife from the kid and press the point of the knife into the lady's forehead. She winces in pain, begging me to stop. It should hurt. I'm not going to stop. Blood appears. I tell the kid to find me a hammer. I inform the lady that if she keeps talking, this steak knife that she should have stabbed me with instead of that baseball bat will be hammered into her skull. She gets quiet but she's still crying. That'll shut her up.

I wonder if I could actually kill this lady. I don't feel

the aggression I usually feel or the adrenaline rush I enjoy in these moments. No heart pounding. Body temperature is normal. Breathing is regular. I'm calm. This feels too easy. I don't have the urge I usually have. I'm just going through the motions to scare her. That's exactly what I'm doing. Keep it up Donovan because it's working.

I can't kill this lady even though she's a piece of shit mom. I don't know her life story but it shouldn't have chapters of being a drugged up, prostitute raising a son in a borderline crack house brothel. When did your life go wrong? Who got you into drugs? Who made you think using your body for money was a smart, healthy, economic decision? How did you afford a house in this neighborhood?

Your son isn't tainted yet. He's blind to all the wrong in your life which is great. The only good thing I see in this house. Jesus lady. Why am I feeling bad for you? I should be panting, foaming out the mouth, screaming at your son to hurry up and bring me a hammer to make this knife destroy your brain because you used it for poor life choices.

The kid comes back with a hammer. I thank him and hold it in my hand, keeping the knife point pressed into her forehead, all for show with no actual performance.

"Where was I? Oh yeah. So this adult performer was doing this interracial scene. That's when two or more people of different races, colors, have sex together. Get it? Good. She was white and the male performer was black. So I'm jacking off, watching them go at it. He fucks every hole on her body. She sucks everything on him. You know what happens in a porno. So I'm enjoying this scene, beating the shit outta my dick, especially when he fucks her in the ass. She has a fat ass and a pretty pink asshole. He's about to bust and do you know what he says?"

I pause for a moment.

"He tells the girl to babysit his motherfucking kids in her motherfucking mouth. I'm like oh shit. Never heard someone say that before. She says okay daddy with no enthusiasm. This isn't going to end well. Then she starts sucking his dick and he cums in her mouth. She's about to swallow and he yells at her, telling her she better not murder his kids. She better babysit them. She opens her mouth in disgust. He yells again, telling her not one of his kids better not fall out of her mouth. I stopped beating my dick. I couldn't believe what I was seeing. She's really babysitting his kids in her motherfucking mouth. I was amazed. She's actually listening to this dude."

"But then she starts crying. A few seconds later she gulps downs all of that man's poor kids. They died soon after in her stomach. Boy was that guy mad. He fucked her and made her do it all over again. I found another porno to watch before he came again. And what made me think of that girl when I see you is that the two of y'all can't handle responsibility. Maybe he wanted his kids back after she babysat them. It wasn't her right to eat them. All she had to do was babysit them for a little while. A porn scene don't last forever. And just like that girl, you can't handle the responsibility when it comes to kids. You can't even handle one child. I bet you eat your client's kids too without permission. Earlier you said that you should have never kept your son. How many abortions does that vagina of yours own? Unlimited? I'm listening."

"You said you'll kill me if I talk."

"Then why did you just utter words?"

"Please." She starts crying loudly. "I'll get my life together."

"I honestly don't care what you do. Just don't hit your son ever again. I'll be around again in case you do. I'm pretty sure he'll let me know. He seems to trust me."

"I won't."

"I hope so. The foster care system has a horrible track record."

"I'll do better."

"You don't have to tell me. You just have to do it."

"Thank you."

"Don't thank me yet. I still have this hammer in my hand and knife poking at your forehead."

I get off of her. I leave the house. The kid follows. The hammer and knife goes in a trash can nearby. I head back to the sister's house. The kid keeps following me with a smile on his face. He begins to talk.

"You're the only man that stood up for me."

"What?"

"You told her to stop hitting me. None of the other men that come over tell her that."

"Oh yeah. Sure. Whatever kid. You're welcome. Why are you following me?"

"You passed the Epic Hero, hero test. Congratulations."

"Thanks?"

"You're welcome. What do you want to be called?"

"Donovan."

"That's not a hero name."

"Well it's either going to be Donovan or Donovan."

"How about Mighty Strong Man?"

"No and somebody needs to teach you how to name a hero."

"Okay Donovan." He says sarcastically. "Thanks for stopping my mom from hitting me."

"Hey, hey, hey kid. Don't get all emotional around me. Save that for your dad."

"But I don't have a dad."

"Exactly."

"When do you want to start fighting crime?"

"Ummm… tomorrow. I gotta make my costume tonight." I lie.

"We wear uniforms, not costumes."

"Whatever you say kid. You can go back home now."

"I don't want to."

"Are you scared?"

"No."

"Well you can't go where I'm going. Sorry kid. Go play with one of your friends."

"You are my only friend."

I stop walking. A feeling inside me emerges. It's feels good. A happy feeling. I should have kept that knife to stab this feeling inside of me. "That sucks kid. I'll see you later. Don't follow me."

I leave the kid.

Bertha greets me at the door before I even knock, wearing a green transparent robe with no makeup. She screams and starts crying. "Brown Bear! Your face!"

I absolutely forgot about my face. It stopped hurting. From Bertha's scream, the kid's mom's nails went to work on my face. "I can't explain Bertha. It's nothing. I just want to lay down and relax."

Bertha grabs me and gives me a huge hug, breasts pressing beautifully against my chest. I grab her ass, my dick growing hard. I'm enjoying the moment but then Bertha starts to sniff me. What is she doing? The hug ends with Bertha pushing me away from her.

"Is that fucking perfume I smell Brown Bear?"

You gotta be fucking kidding me.

That lady fucking stunk.

12

"Brown Bear you got five seconds to tell me why you smell like perfume and why that beautiful face of yours is scratched up. I got a million different horror stories going on in my head that's breaking my heart of what you've been up to and I need to know the actual story before I go insane and bite your fucking dick off."

I'm sitting on the couch in the living room as Bertha looks down upon me, crying, her makeup ruined from her tears. I was staring at her boobs, enjoying their presence, until she mentioned removing my dick from my body with her mouth.

Bertha looks devastated and hurt. This is the second time that I haven't done anything wrong but something inside of Bertha's brain tells her that I have spent my time outside of the house cheating on her which is beyond false. I think silicone ruins the brain.

Thankfully located in neither of Bertha's hands is a gun. She put it away. Thank God. She has killed too many men who have broken her heart and I'm not trying to be the next for an imaginary crime I've never committed.

"First off I would like to say how much I love-"

"Brown Bear if you try to sweet talk me or try to justify being unfaithful to me, I'm going to take my gun, shove it inside of your dick hole, and use your dick as a silencer as I shoot holes throughout your insides," Bertha says as Wendy walks into the room with the gun, handing it to her sister.

Oh my fucking God I'm never leaving this house again.

"Bertha, listen. I was hanging out with this kid and I met his mom and-"

"So that's who you was fucking. A kid's mom." Bertha points the gun in my face. Her eyes, face angry and pissed.

"Oh my God Bertha would you please listen."

"Go ahead. Explain. Wendolynn go in the kitchen and get me a cheese grater."

"You sure Bertha?"

"Get me that cheese grater Wendolynn. Talk Brown Bear."

Get to the point. She's ready to kill you Donovan. I can't do anything right.

"The kid's mom was about to hit him so I stopped her but in the process she spit in my face, clawed me and that's the reason why my face looks the way it does."

A huge gasp and look of surprised disgust is made by Bertha with my statement. Then her look goes angry again. "Somebody hurt you?"

"What?"

"That bitch hurt you?"

What? "I don't get it. You was just crying when you saw my face earlier. What did you think happened to my face? You think I fell or something. You think sex did this somehow to my face?"

"Don't get smart with me Brown Bear. You could have forced yourself onto her unwillingly."

"What? I'm not some kind of monster! The kid's mom clawed at my face to escape."

"Escape what?"

"I was on top of her to try to-" This isn't sounding good at all.

Fuck.

"She hits her son, does drugs, and runs a single lady brothel in her house."

"Should I shoot you now Brown Bear because you just told me you were on top of a prostitute."

"Bertha, everything I say isn't going to sound good." Oh my God Donovan say something that isn't going to get you killed. "She is a terrible mom and I was trying to scare her straight. I was ready to kill her."

"Prove it."

"I think my face is enough proof. Her forehead is pierced from the knife I was ready to hammer into her head."

Wendy walks into the room.

"Here is the cheese grater Bertha."

"Place it on the coffee table, Wendolynn."

"Whatever you say Bertha." Wendy says, placing the cheese grater on the coffee table right next to me. She looks at me and shakes her head.

I didn't do anything.

"Prove it Brown Bear."

Did she not just hear what I said? I tell this lady the truth and it blows right by her. It's like Bertha's brain puts everything I do involving violence inflicted on other people in her bullshit brain folder. "How can I prove it Bertha?"

"Pull them down. Show him to me."

"What?" Wasn't expecting that. So my confession is filed in her bullshit folder. Bertha still thinks I had sex with that disgusting example of a lady. The thought of me having sex with that kid's mom is disgusting. Her vagina would probably melt the condom to my dick or even worse, my penis would disintegrates to nothing once it enters inside her. None of this would ever happen because the sight of the kid's mom makes my penis micro.

"NOW!" Bertha screams, making me jump in shock.

"Okay, okay. Relax." I get up and whip my dick out cautiously.

Bertha gets on her knees and inspects my cock. He's fully erect. Bertha smells my cock, tasting it also with her tongue, checking for any evidence of sexual juices not belonging to her.

Every time she sees an area on my cock that catches her

attention, she touches it with her gun, moving my dick skin which causes my heart to pound violently. I can't get an idea of what's going through her head since I can't see her face. All I see is her short red hair. I'm so thankful right now that my cock didn't start pre-cumming. Bertha might mistake that for leftover cum from my imaginary fuck session and actually murder my dick with her mouth.

How did my life come to this?

My balls are next to inspect. The inspection ends soon after.

"I believe you Brown Bear." Bertha kisses my balls. "Your pretty balls feel fuller than when I last felt on them earlier." She gets up, grabs my cheeks, pressing them together forcibly with the hand not holding the gun, causing my wounds to sting. "Don't you ever scare me again Brown Bear."

My balls are probably swollen from you squeezing them to near bursting earlier.

"Noted. I'll never cheat on you Bertha. You're the only one-"

"Is she still alive?"

"Yes."

"Who is she and where does she live?"

"I don't know her name and she lives like two blocks down the street."

"What does she look like Brown Bear?"

"Shit. She looks like drugs were her mother and father."

"Oh that bitch. I know exactly who she is Brown Bear. I'll be back." Bertha kisses me, smiles, then leaves the house.

My description must have been perfect. Great job Donovan. I pull my pants up.

Wendy is staring at me smiling. She has on a blue, form fitting dress. Her curves are showcased as usual with anything the sisters decide to wear. Seeing Wendy, Bertha's twin, so calm, sweet, natural, and laid back makes me wonder if the gallons of silicon plays a part in Bertha's craziness. Is silicon poisonous at all? Was Bertha ever anything like Wendy? The photos around the house say that they were once similar, look wise but the photos fail in telling me if they were similar, personality wise.

"Your sister is something else."

"She'll say the same thing about you."

"What do you think?"

"I think you're exactly what you're supposed to be. The same for my sister."

"You don't think she's a little crazy?"

"Everyone a little crazy Donovan. Could you imagine a world if everyone wasn't?"

I think for a moment. "No." Everyone is a little bit crazy. Some more than others. I wonder what's crazy about Wendy. "What's crazy about you?"

"Where do I start? Let me think."

Shit.

"Stop playing. You don't need to think."

"Hold on."

"Okay." She does have to think. Please don't be crazy like Bertha.

"Okay. Here is one of the craziest things I ever did. My third boyfriend Frederick was cheating on me."

This is going to be good. I should have popped some popcorn. What is up with these sisters with their cheating boyfriends and lovers? Wendy and Bertha are borderline perfect in their separate ways. I hope unfaithfulness doesn't equal death in Wendy's world.

"Frederick made the mistake of planning a date with me the same day and time of this tramp he was messing around with. He had to choose which one of us to cancel on. Unfortunately for him he chose me. Told me he had to work part of the night shift. Typical man bullshit. So I played stupid. I played along. He came home around four in the morning. Freddy use to like to keep a bottle of soda beside the bed. So I put a few sleeping pills in the soda. As expected, he drinks the soda when he lays in bed and a little while later, falls asleep."

"I strip him naked and tie him up to the bedposts. I bought a bottle of lighter fluid and a few rolls of aluminum foil. Before tying him up to the bedpost, I covered the bed to the best of my ability with the aluminum foil I bought. As he was tied up, I emptied the lighter fluid on his private parts and inside his mouth. He stayed asleep during all this. He finally awoke once I tossed a matched in his mouth. Poor Frederick. All you had to do was be faithful to me. He kept letting the lighter fluid leak out his mouth. Got all over his face and eyes. You ever see eyes burn before Donovan? It isn't pretty."

"Once I lit his privates on fire, his body went berserk. Freddy started shaking profusely. His right arm managed to break out of the tie. He was smacking the hell out of his penis and balls to try to stop the fire. More worried about his manhood than his burning face. Typical man. It was pointless though. I soaked his penis and balls in lighter fluid. I basically marinated his private parts in lighter fluid. The fire took about six minutes to kill him. I watched the whole thing, Frederick's constant flailing threw the lighter fluid everywhere from his mouth. I miss him sometimes. I think about him occasionally."

I'm living with monsters.

That was a lot to process.

I'm living with psychopaths.

The entire time Wendy talked, there was no doubt in my mind that she wasn't lying. Her eyes stayed focused, looking at memories only she can see. Memories a former lover of Wendy's once experienced. Memories that I never wish to experience from Wendy or her sister Bertha.

Memories Bertha and Wendy can commit but somehow I can't.

I'm a joke.

"So you and Bertha can do all this terrible stuff to people but when I mention myself doing it, which I actually do, it's impossible in you and your sister's eyes."

Laughter echoes from Wendy's mouth. "You don't have to make up horror stories to fit in with us Donovan. We like you just the way you are."

"But they're true."

"Sure they are."

Laughable and impossible as always Donovan. Can't they see I'm a killer since they are? Shouldn't killers have an eye for a fellow killer? Better yet, shouldn't these psycho sisters be worried that I don't flinch when they tell me these vengeful tales? They should be surprised that I haven't ran and told the authorities on them. That should tell them something.

"It doesn't alarm you or your sister that I haven't went to the cops with all the stuff you and your sister have told me and the things your sister did to me? Bertha loves to threaten my life."

"Never thought about it. Bertha mentioned something to me the other day about you being too scared to leave her."

"I'm not."

"That could explain why you haven't left. You're too scared to leave."

"But I'm not. Maybe it's because I do stuff just like y'all two."

"Here you go again."

"I'm serious."

"Tell me about one then."

"I set the Pastor on fire."

"Creative. I tell you about setting someone on fire and coincidently you have done the same. So convenient Donovan."

"Forget it."

"Awww, poor Donovan. I'm sorry." She starts laughing again. "Come here."

"No."

"I'll let you touch my big juicy tits."

"No."

"Donovan, why do you want to be like us so bad?"

Why? Because I am. Because I feel so alive being the reason their skull is crushed. Because I'm the reason he'll never see tomorrow. Because my body ignites with adrenaline and heart pounds with ecstasy only from such wicked acts. I control if someone continues to live or not.

"It doesn't matter. You'll never believe me."

"How can I cheer you up Donovan? I don't want Bertha coming back and seeing you like this. She'll kill me if she knew I have any part in your sadness."

"I'm good."

"I think my tits would like some attention," Wendy's says while pulling out her breasts.

Dammit Wendy. I grab her breasts and start softly rubbing, kissing, and sucking on her natural breasts. It's rare I get to do this with Wendy alone. I remember doing this only once before with her. Every other time it is together with Wendy and Bertha and Bertha throws a fit if I touch or fuck her sister a little too long or get a little too passionate with Wendy in the bedroom. It feels good to be able to enjoy something natural every once in a while. A taste of reality is well appreciated. Humbling in a sense to get a taste of both worlds. Natural and exotic. Both under the same roof.

We fuck. Wendy knows it's fucking. I grab her shoulders forcefully as I hit it from the back doggy style. She's different from Bertha. Wendy likes to get right to fucking or what Bertha likes to call love making. I think she knows I belong to Bertha so she doesn't waste time with foreplay. Wendy told me once that foreplay is what couples do. So me and Bertha are a couple I guess. A very odd one at that.

I don't have a choice.

I'm her prisoner.

I'm in prison again.

Stop complaining Donovan.

I cum a while after. She did twice if I remember correctly. I hop in the shower first. We don't lie together sweaty and cuddle in bed after sex because that's what couples do. I can dig it. I'm surprised she doesn't have a male companion. She caught my eye before Bertha did. Wendy is calmer than Bertha personality-wise.

Bertha lets me know every time she was ready to kill me. Wendy probably would wait before quietly killing me or put sleeping pills in my drink and then set my dick, balls, and mouth on fire. In another world I would be Wendy's Brown Bear but she would hopefully call me Donovan. She'll call me Donovan. No daily guns to my face. A guy can dream can't he? With either sister death by their hands is a high possibility. It's a lose-lose situation with either sister.

I'm crazy if I stay here.

I should run away.

No.

"I'm heading out." I tell Wendy when I'm done getting dressed.

"I don't think my sister is going to let you live if you cheat on her a third time Donovan."

"Don't tell me you actually believe I cheat."

"I believe what Bertha believes."

"I should be dead then."

"Maybe Bertha decided to give you three strikes. I would after all the guys she killed after they cheated once. You already have two strikes. If you didn't cheat you did a terrible job convincing her you didn't."

"She's pretty hard to convince."

"If your life is on the line Donovan, you better be awfully convincing."

"Thanks for the advice."

Wendy replies with a smile.

Smart bitch. I leave the house.

It takes a few knocks before Mr. Worthy comes to the

door. He yawns and greets me with a surprised look. He must have been sleeping. His breath smells unclean. I start talking.

"I saw some guy acting weird like an hour ago."

That wakes him right up. "Where? Why didn't you stop by sooner?"

"I was following him around. Let me in. I'll tell you what he looks like."

"Sure sure. Come inside."

This is one lonely old man. House is extremely clean with no signs of a wife or kids. No pets. Absolutely nothing is out of place. All the newspapers he has on the coffee table are folded, stacked, and recent. The only thing wrong with this place is his breath.

He tells me to take a seat on the couch that looks brand new. I sit down and Mr. Worthy does too soon after. I'm surprised he allows meetings and prayers in his house. There are no signs of human activity in here. The only thing that you can see that shows that he holds neighborhood watch meetings in his home is the bulletin board he has neatly filled with information of suspects and night watch routes throughout the neighborhood.

A picture of me is posted on the board. That isn't good. Paranoid old man.

"So tell me about the man you saw." Mr. Worthy asks, pulling out a pen and notepad from his pocket.

"He was a man."

"You told me that already. I need to know race."

"He was white."

"Good. What else?"

I think of some bullshit. "He wore a cut off jean jacket with ripped up jeans. He wore a white t-shirt with a picture on it of a red hand giving the middle finger. His hair was blonde and long. He had a handlebar mustache."

"Excellent. It has been a while since my neighborhood watch group has had any suspicious activity to watch out for. Sorry about when we first met. I can't ignore suspicious people in this neighborhood. I have to keep the children safe."

"No need to apologize. Just glad you didn't arrest me." I force myself to laugh.

Ha.

"I've done it before."

"You told me last time we talked."

"You haven't told the authorities about this man have you?"

"No sir."

"Excellent. The neighborhood watch will handle this matter."

"You sure?"

"Certainly. I've been keeping this neighborhood safe for close to thirty years son."

"I believe you."

"Now where is this guy at?"

"I'm not too sure." Make up some more bullshit. "Last time I seen him he was in the bushes."

"I'm not understanding son. What bushes?"

"About three blocks away."

"Son just about-"

"My name is Donovan."

"Mr. Gold, just about every house has bushes in the front."

"Oh yeah. Well I stopped following him once I seen he had a gun in his back pocket."

"Jesus. This guy sounds like trouble. We'll have to start our walk a little early this evening."

"Sounds good."

"Would you care joining us? We could always use the extra help."

"Yeah whatever. I'll be there tonight."

"Excellent."

"Yeah. Do you have any water?"

"I most certainly do. In the fridge, third shelf from the bottom. You'll see a couple bottles as soon as you open the door."

"I'll be back." I head into the kitchen.

I grab a knife from a drawer in the kitchen. It's serrated. Instead of getting a water bottle, I spend that time thinking of a way to end Mr. Worthy. Slitting his throat would be too easy. I could stab him to death but if I wanted to do that I could have just gotten a regular knife from the knife block on the kitchen counter.

I don't plan on serrating him to death. That's not exhilarating at all. Pointless knife. I place it back in the drawer but another item catches my attention. A silver meat mallet lays in the drawer. How did I not notice this a few seconds ago? I can have a ton of fun with this. I head back to the living room.

The couch is facing away from the kitchen. I walk slowly so Mr. Worthy doesn't hear me returning. I get the feeling that I haven't felt since my trip at the pizza shop. I miss this feeling. It has been so long.

Hello old friend.

Oh this meat mallet is going to bring me joy. The feeling is overwhelming but welcomed. If only my trip with the Pastor didn't go bad and take forever to happen. What could have been.

I'm behind Mr. Worthy. He's patiently waiting for me to return, totally unaware that a meat mallet is lifted above his head, ready to tenderize parts of his body, turning his bones into sand, flesh into mush.

Gunshots erupt from a distance, startling me. Startled, the meat mallet drops from my hands, falling under the couch. Mr. Worthy pops up from his seat in a defensive stance. More gunshots erupt. Mr. Worthy runs into another room in his house. I get down on my stomach and feel for the mallet under the couch. Dammit Donovan. I can't feel it.

Mr. Worthy runs back into the room, wearing his leather

jacket. He heads for the door.

"Don't forget to lock the door on your way out."

I stand up. "What are you doing?"

"I'm going to arrest that bastard!"

"He has a gun Mr. Worthy?"

"So do I." Mr. Worthy says, pulling out a sawed off shotgun from the inside of his jacket, smiling, putting it back, and then leaving the house.

Oh shit.

I take a seat on the couch. I made up the gunman in the jean clothes. It had to be crazy Bertha pulling that trigger. Dammit Bertha. I was seconds away from an amazing time in this house. Oh what could have been.

Sadness erupts inside from amazing events that'll never become reality, only thoughts in my head. Dammit Donovan. Next time run up to that motherfucker with the meat mallet and use his head as a piñata.

I head home disappointed. I'm pissed. Walking home I see a couple kids along the way. I greet each of them with Mr. Middle Finger. Fuck you, you stupid kids. I kicked one who got too close to me. One kid had a lollipop in their mouth and I pulled that shit out of his mouth and I tossed the fuck outta that shit. Fuck you kid. Fuck you lollipop.

As I return to the front of the house, I see Bertha turning the corner, heading back also, gun held in her damn hand. That fucking gun.

"Dammit Bertha!" I yell at her furiously.

"What's wrong Brown Bear?" She asks confusingly. "Somebody hurt you again?"

"You're always fucking something up! Why did you have to kill her?"

"Don't you dare raise your voice at me Brown Bear!" She points that stupid gun to my face. "Why? Because she marked up something that is mine. You have a problem with that Brown Bear? Y'all had something going on between y'all two? Do you want me to pull this trigger?"

"You're not *FUCKING* listening Bertha." The gun doesn't frighten me anymore. "I was doing something really important and you being trigger happy with that fucking gun ruined it. Now get that gun outta my fucking face before I get mad."

"Oh Brown Bear. What took you so long to talk to me that way? You got me all wet with your stern voice and demeanor. Why don't you take me inside and fuck me?"

"Oh my goodness Bertha! I was in the process of killing someone and you fucked it up by you killing someone."

"Here you go again."

"Listen! I'm serious right now."

"Sure you are."

"I am."

"So are you going to slide that thick cock inside my pussy and fuck me stupid or not?"

"Bertha can't you tell I'm mad at you right now!"

"That's why I want you to fuck me and not make love to me."

"Dammit Bertha!"

She always wins.

"Now let's go inside before a cop drives by and sees me with this gun."

My penis is sore, balls shrunken to peas. Bertha is an animal in the bedroom when it should be me. She can go on and on and on. She doesn't even break a sweat either.

She sits on the edge of the bed, naked, beautiful. A pleased and beautiful champion in the bedroom. I lay in the bed hurt, defeated, and drained. Her beautiful assets are hidden from my sight with a silk sheet. I think she's trying to tease me. She never covers herself up. This lady is heaven sent. I take a nap.

I awake all alone in the bedroom. My legs hurt from cramping from our last bedroom session. She likes to go at it even harder during and after my climax. The feeling is pleasantly maddening. My legs tend to tense up a little too much. I roll out of bed.

The house is empty. Good. I walk around naked. I make myself a turkey and cheese sandwich. I enjoy the delicious sandwich while standing up in the kitchen, admiring my physique from what I can see appearing on the chrome fridge. I wonder how well Bertha and Wendy's sandwich making skills are. They should be extravagant. They are both mature in age. Hopefully their skills matured too. From what they can do in the bedroom, their sandwiches must keep a man's mouth watering for more. Gotta get them to make me a few sometime.

Nothing good is on TV. I check the clock in the living room. It's close to midnight. Where did the sisters go? I fondle myself for a while thinking of Bertha and Wendy. I'm horny again and my penis feels like it's been tortured. Yeah, tortured by sex and more sex. I can hardly walk with a boner. The soreness hurts too much.

I walked back into the kitchen to make another sandwich to relieve my boner. I have to get my mind off the sisters and their sexual magic. I head for the fridge, and from a window I struggle for a second but make out the face of the kid staring at me angrily while my penis is still rock hard pointing at him.

This fucking kid.

I put boxers on and meet him outside.

"Jeez kid! Thanks for being super creepy."

"You're no hero."

"What are you talking about kid?"

"You hired the hit on my mom. You had her killed."

"What? That's nonsense."

"I was there. I saw her murdered."

Holy shit Bertha! What the fuck is wrong with you lady. In front of her son? Oh man.

"You saw the whole thing?"

"Everything."

"You don't seem too bummed out kid." He just has that

stupid angry child look every stupid angry child has.

"A hero can never be fazed. I will have justice from what that fat lady did to my mom."

"First of all, she isn't fat. She's actually thick. You'll learn to like thick women once your balls drop. You'll crave them. Second, justice? How?"

"You'll see."

"Whatever you say. And if it means anything I didn't hire the hit on your mom. Karma did kid."

"The fat lady Karma will pay."

"Wait, what? No. Karma is when something… never mind. Yeah Karma will pay." I gotta remember he's like… damn I don't even know how old he is. He told me before I think.

"My new name is Epic Hero Lone Wolf."

"You sure you wasn't alone before kid?"

"Shut up and follow me."

This kid. I put on more clothes.

We're in someone's backyard. It's too dark to tell whose backyard we're trespassing in. I have no clue. I barely know a small percentage of people in this neighborhood. Maybe the kid knows. I don't bother to ask.

The grass hasn't been taken care of in some time. The inground pool that I just almost fell into is basically a huge dumpster now. Fencing around this yard is non-existent except the few wooden posts scattered around the perimeter of the yard. This kid sure knows where the shittiest places around this neighborhood are. I guess when you grow up in shit, you'll always know where to find more. I surprised I haven't noticed this yard when I walk around the neighborhood.

The kid motions me with his hand to follow him. He's walking while crouched, stealth style. He surely believes he's some type of hero. We head for the backdoor of the house. It's locked. I go to knock on it and I'm instantly dragged down to the kid's level by my arm.

"What was that for?"

"Shut up and listen. They have guns in there."

"How do you know?"

"I saw them in there."

"How?"

"I was in there before."

"Do you know these people? This family?"

"They are villains. Bad guys. They make white powder in there. I have to find out what their plans are with the white powder. I think it's poison or toxic powder."

I try hard not to laugh.

They are villains. Bad guys.

No.

They are drug dealers kid. I try to keep a serious face. The kid has found the local drug house. Trap house. This kid should be the head of the neighborhood watch. The kid sure does know how to find the filth in this neighborhood. I have too many questions to ask this kid.

"How did you get in there?"

"I found a way."

Smartass. "Then let's go."

"It's gone."

"What happened to your way in?"

"Something happened last time."

"What happened? You got in trouble? They hurt you? Come on now kid. Spit it out."

"They caught me and kicked me out."

"That's it?"

"Yes."

"What did you expect? They're grownups and you're a little kid sneaking into their place."

"A hero should never be caught."

"Well you got caught kid. Suck it up."

"We must stop them."

"We?"

"Yes."

"No."

"You're a coward."

Me? Donovan a coward? Please kid. How should I convince this kid to not walk into this place a second time? An idea ignites in my mind. "Are you positive kid that they are not just making baby powder?"

"Yes."

"How?"

"I got baby powder in my nose before. That's not baby powder in there."

Everyone around me is crazy. "What made you do that?"

"Some of the bad guys in the house was sniffing the powder."

I knew it. Fuck. Well if he witnessed the people sniffing the powder then he should know that it isn't poison or toxic in the way the kid is thinking poison and toxic.

"Did you like it?"

"Shut up. My mom laughed at me and called me an idiot."

Is that idiotic for a kid to do? The two do look similar. "Didn't you see what happened after they sniffed the powder?"

"No."

"No?"

"I got kicked out remember."

"Oh yeah. Well I can tell you what happens. You get really high and your heart pumps fast. The end. Now let's go before someone sees us. I'm not trying to be murdered tonight."

"You're lying."

"Me?"

"Yes."

"Alright kid. There is something you're not telling me. You were in this house for like a second before you were caught and kicked out. So what else did you see in there?"

"Nothing."

"You're losing me here kid. There is nothing else to see in there. You saw everything. Guns, people, and cocaine."

"Justice needs to be brought into this house."

"But why kid?"

He drags me over to the pool. The kid points to a corner of the pool where the moon's light barely illuminates upon three bodies lying motionless. The kid informs me that each one of these bodies sniffed the powder the day he was in this house.

"I found them here a few days ago."

"Kid I really think we should leave here."

"No."

"Well I'm leaving."

"Coward."

"Whatever you say kid."

"The powder probably turned them into zombies so they had to be killed. I have to stop this."

"Why aren't you a zombie then kid?"

"I only took a little. They took a lot."

"Kid you're searching for an adventure that doesn't exist. I'm leaving. You should to."

Before I leave I take a closer look at the bodies. They are located on the shallow end of the pool. Once in their proximity, their sour, rotten smell turns my stomach upside down. I hold back vomit. Each one of these people have a bullet hole in their head. Oh I know what happened. These three dead idiots did something they weren't supposed to do.

Big mistake. Death is their new reality.

Simple. Kids and their crazy imagination.

I look for the kid. He's not anywhere I'm looking. I look at the house and there is a small silhouette on the roof of the house opening up a window. I run to the house.

"Hey!" I whisper loudly to the kid.

He ignores me.

"Get down from there."

Nothing.

"The powder didn't kill those people. Those people's people killed them."

"Liar." I hear the kid whisper under his breath.

Stupid kid.

"Let me help you."

"I thought you were leaving."

"You need my help."

"How?"

"We need a plan."

"I already have one."

"You're going to get yourself killed."

"So what."

So what? This kid is ruthless. "Come on kid. Come down here and let's make a plan together before you get yourself hurt. You need me kid."

"We will make a plan in the house after I open the backdoor for you." He goes through the window.

Fuck.

13

"Kid either you're the bravest two year old I've ever seen or you don't know how to properly use that brain inside your head." I say to the kid in a dark hallway inside the house.

"I thought we were going to make a plan."

"We are kid but-"

"If you're going to try and prevent me from doing the right thing, then you can leave. It's not happening. I'm not leaving."

I just want to rip his stupid green cape off and take off those stupid red gloves and burn them. This hero bullshit is rotting his mind. "Kid these people are murderers."

"Good thing I have this." The kid says while revealing to me a pistol in his hand.

"Where the fuck did you get that?" My heart starts to pound.

"It was on the bed in a room upstairs."

"I thought you were a hero? Heroes don't kill."

"It's for you. You're the one who's afraid. Epic Hero Lone Wolf isn't afraid of anything."

This fucking kid.

"You need a fucking ass whooping kid. Trying to save the neighborhood and shit one drug house at a time. I didn't sign up for this bullshit."

"I didn't make you sign anything."

"Figure of speech kid. Now listen. How many people do you think are in this house right now other than us?"

"Two."

"How do you know?" He sounded too confident in his response.

"I saw two people upstairs."

"What! Did they see you like last time? Shit kid."

"No. I don't make mistakes twice."

"Kid this whole thing is a fucking mistake. Where are they?"

"Someone is in the bathroom upstairs and a man is sleeping."

"Okay. Now what was your plan kid?"

"Arrest them. They're bad guys. Killers."

"That's it? We're not cops."

"We could tie them up then call the cops."

"Tie them up with what kid? Air? Our shoe strings?"

"You don't have to be mean to me." The kid's tough guy ego starts to fade. "You got a better idea?"

"Yes I most certainly do. We leave this house and never come back so we don't end up with bullet holes in our heads. I love living kid."

"Coward. You're no hero."

"I know. I'm Donovan."

"You should change your name to Coward. Mr. Coward."

"Cheer up kid. Now let's go."

"You gotta put the gun back."

"I don't have to do anything."

"I took it from the man's hand who was sleeping."

"What! You're fucking insane kid."

"A hero always disarms the bad guys."

"So you just took it from him in his sleep and that's it?"

"Yes."

"You didn't knock him out or nothing?"

"No."

Upstairs someone yells at someone else about their missing gun. A bed squeaks. Footsteps echo throughout the house from upstairs. Two people argue over a missing gun. One of the people arguing informs the other person that he'll get beat the fuck up if his gun isn't found. Guy tells other guy to go ask Ricky.

A third person upstairs?

My blood starts to boil. Just sprint out of the house Donovan. Take the kid with you. Drag him by his stupid cape too. I'm starting to hate this kid.

A guy screams *"RICKY WHERE IS MY FUCKING GUN"*.

Ricky replies "I don't fucking know Don. Ask Jack."

Don tells Ricky "I just fucking asked Jack".

"Then I don't fucking know" responds Ricky.

"I spent over twelve hundred dollars on that gun."

"Then get the fuck outta bed and push more weight. You should have plenty of guns by now but you always sleeping instead of pushing weight you sleepy ass bitch."

"Fuck you Ricky."

"It had to be that kid." Jack announces.

"Kid?" Ricky and Don both say confused.

"That little kid that always comes in here. He wears that stupid cape."

"I'm going to kill that mother fucker!"

"Yeah go ahead Don. Kill a five year old kid. Fucking bitch."

They continue to argue.

"You're killing me kid. We can't leave now. They'll come for you. You snuck in here before more than once. And you call me a liar."

"I'm just doing the duties of a hero."

"By failing and failing and failing and failing but constantly trying to stop drug dealers. Kid what the fuck?"

"I'm not scared."

"You don't have to be because scared or not, a bullseye is permanently tattooed on you."

"What's the plan?"

"Plan? There is no fucking plan kid. What should happen now is we place this gun on the ground and run home."

"No."

"Well bye. See you later kid."

"I'll scream."

"Go ahead. Scream you little shit. I'll break your legs so they won't have to chase after you before they kill you."

"You were never hero material. I'll finish this." The kid walks away and towards the direction of the steps.

"Alright. Where is the damn kitchen around here?"

"Why?"

"I need a weapon."

"Take the gun."

"Heroes don't use guns kid."

"Cops do."

"Cops aren't heroes kid. They're cops."

"You're not a hero."

"Just show me where the stupid fucking kitchen is kid."

"It's this way."

I follow the kid.

The whole time talking and trying to reason with the kid, I found myself asking myself numerous times in the back of my head why this kid is still in my presence and massively influencing my decisions. I should have kick this kid to the curb days ago. I should be getting my balls lathered up by Bertha's mouth juices. I should have my hands around someone's neck knowing that I'll be the one that'll live to see tomorrow. But here I am with a steak knife in each hand, heart thumping, body on fire and sweaty, about to sneak upstairs to kill three men before I'm caught and the kid is caught for the millionth time.

All this for three reasons. One, the kid being the sneaking prick that he is, saw me murder the Pastor. Two, the kid has an issue with trying to make the world a better place. And three, I got this horrible feeling deep down for this kid. I think the feeling is called caring or compassion and I absolutely fucking hate it. I think compassion is going to get me killed tonight. Fucking feelings.

Can you physically kill compassion?

"Just put it back."

"Kid I'm not going to just go up there and put a murder weapon back into a murderer's hands. What comic books do you be reading? What hero does that?"

"You're not a hero."

"I'm also not an idiot. Now wait down here so I can give those guys upstairs some 'justice.'"

"I want to see."

"Trust me you do not want to see what I'm about to do."

"You're going to kill them."

"No I'm not. I going to arrest them so justice can be served to them."

"I don't believe you."

"Nobody does. Now stay down here."

"Why are you holding knives?"

"I'm going to arrest them."

"Cops don't use knives."

"I do."

"Why are you shaking so much?"

Excitement. The moment before the rush. "You wouldn't understand kid."

"You're scared."

"I'm beyond alive."

I slowly walk up the steps. Creaking comes from the wooden stairs but inaudible for the drug dealers to hear over their yelling. I stop when I get to the top of the steps. The dealers sound separated, yelling from different rooms. Okay Donovan. What would you rather be doing? Please don't die tonight Donovan. Sex after this with Bertha would be the greatest day in the life and times of Donovan.

Don't die you fucking bitch.

I check the closest room with sound coming from it. The door is already open and I slowly peek in the room enough to not be noticed. A television is the cause of the sound. Fucking television. Fuck you. I give the television the finger.

A toilet flushing alarms me from behind. There's a bathroom behind me with a person in it. The fun is finally about to start. I stand directly in front of the door. Oh the feeling of being in control of life or death. The door starts to open. I hold in my smile and joy and become rage.

One knife enters his throat. He's looks so confused. Aren't we all? He grabs onto my hand. You are too late sir. There's a knife already in your neck. I end his confusion with another knife through his forehead. His body loses all purpose. I help the body slowly to the ground to not attract any unwanted attention to the bathroom. I don't think this asshole washed his hands and he touched me. That's nasty.

I take some time but I manage to remove the knife from his forehead. The one in his throat was easy. The bathroom floor is painted red with what use to flow throughout his veins. It's crazy how red blood is. It's like red red.

Two voices are still yelling at each other from different rooms. I'm standing in the tub behind the shower curtain. I'm burning up.

Hey guys, come find your dead friend.

I flush the toilet five or six times to attract attention to the bathroom. It doesn't work. Stupid fucking toilet. All this arguing over a gun. I grow tired of waiting. I hate waiting. I leave the bathroom.

There are weird noises coming from this one room. I sneak closer to the door and the noises become less weird and more sexual. Sex noises. People are having sex in a room. A girl is moaning. What the fuck kid. The amount of people upstairs are growing by the minute. Okay Donovan. So there is a lady in there fucking someone. I cannot kill a lady because I'm not a monster.

I'm at a crossroads.

I could kill the guy in there but the lady will see my face. I could leave them two alone to their fucking because I wouldn't want anyone to bother me fucking somebody except for another lady that wants to join. Dammit Donovan.

Stay focused. Bertha will kill you if you have the slightest scent of another woman on you. I should leave these two fuckers alone and finish the other two guys but the pervert in me would like to see some ass and titties.

I slowly start to open the door. Now I hear another girl moaning. Oh shit. I'm in luck. I get too excited and just swing the door wide open, hitting the wall with the door. To my horror and disappointment, I'm staring at a black male beating his erect penis to some lesbian porn. I enter, slamming the door behind me.

Someone yells from the distance to "Stop slamming the fucking doors."

Sorry.

"Who the fuck is you homie? You some type of faggot? My dick is out. Get the fuck outta here."

"Oh my God." I say sadly. "I'm beyond disappointed right not. Pull your pants up. I can't kill you like this. I should have never came in here."

"The fuck homie?" The guy says as he stands up, pulling up his pants.

"Thanks."

He looks downs and notices the steak knives I'm holding and blood on my clothes. His eyes fearfully widen. Took him long enough.

"What the fuck happened to you?"

"It's been a long night."

I walk closer to him. I'm close enough to strike now. I pause for a moment before I swipe towards his throat.

Idiotic move.

He doesn't pause and his fist connects squarely on my chin. My legs collapse beneath me. I'm rocked. I'm seeing stars. I hit the ground hard. Fists connect and continue to smash into my face. Darkness is surrounding me.

No!

Something wet is falling, covering my face.

Am I drowning?

What? The punching stopped.

Blood. I taste it. He must have opened a gash over my eyes. Busted my lip. There is so much blood over me. My eyes are close to being shut. From what's left of my vision I see red. Everything is red. Why did the punching stop? I slowly move my head. My head is throbbing. Ringing too. I'm still a little dazed. Where did that guy go? Oh there you are. Wait a second. Why are you lying next to me?

He's barely breathing. I find the strength to pick myself off of the ground. I stumble and hit the ground hard again. I'm rocked. Dizzy. Lay here for a second Donovan. Why is there so much blood?

Am I dying?

What happened again?

Where am I? My head hurts.

I see a man lying across from me. He's not breathing. What the fuck? He has blood all over him. What the fuck happened? I have blood all over myself. The fuck is going on? I try getting up. It's difficult but I stand. My head is pounding. I find something to wipe all this blood off my face. Porn is playing on a computer on the desk. I remember that. I didn't want to see porn. I wanted to see actual ass and titties in front of me. I look at the dead guy and it all comes back to me. How did you die?

His bicep and triceps on his right arm is sliced badly. I inspect further. If not for the bones in his arm I would have sliced his arm off. Wait what? How did I do that? Oh wait. I swiped with my right hand at his throat and he swung at me with his right. Freak event occurred. Freak event saved my life.

Never pause or hesitate again Donovan.

My head!

Why am I doing this again?

I don't hear yelling any more from the other room. No. Why no arguing now? Wait. I hear a TV playing. Man, my head hurts. I look at the body on the floor. I just wanted to see some ass and titties man. I pick up my steak knives and slowly head to the door so I can kill those two guys. I'm not feeling this shit no more. Fuck all this. I want some ass and titties now.

I head out the door. From what I can barely see through my swollen eyes, someone is opening the bathroom door. The fire inside me ignites my adrenaline again. Don't wait Donovan. No pause. No hesitation. No stupid conversation.

Go.

I sprint towards him while he's distracted, shocked, horrified, looking at his dead homie. The blades enter into his neck at an angle. He gasps but that's all the sound that leaves his mouth before the blood does. I push him gently so he collapses on the bathroom floor. He's attempting but failing to survive. He's too weak to remove the blades. Blood leaves his body too quickly. To go from everything to nothing. It's a sight to see.

One last person to end. I'm starting to forget why I'm doing this. I know I like doing it. The rush. I know it has something to do with the kid. The thumping in my head is making it hard for me to think. The pain. This last guy is going to pay for this.

Why am I even in this house?

I kick in the closed door. An obvious black guy is sitting down watching a basketball game on the TV. He jumps up to the sound of the door being kicked opened. He isn't husky. Thank fucking God. The little things in life. The sight of blood all over me shocks him even more than my uninvited entrance. Jaw dropping he runs towards the bed in the room. He falls from his pants sagging to his knees. When will they ever learn. I hurry over to him, not running because my head is ruined.

The knife enters his left hand with a great deal of force, pinning it down into the floor. Screams release from his mouth. The sound is beautiful for a second, then increases the pain in my skull.

"Shut up!" I tell him. I sit down next to him. I'm seeing stars occasionally. Please don't black out you bitch.

"Please don't kill me."

"Too late for that. You're homie in the other room beat the shit outta me. Someone has to pay."

"I go two little girls man."

"Dude. Shut up. Give me a second to relax. You ever had a concussion before? Play football? Concussion?" I close my eyes. The light hurts.

He moans a response.

"You think your little hand hurts. A ton of bricks just fell on my head a little while ago."

No answer. Just more moans.

I look over and he's reaching for the bed. "What are you doing man?"

More moans.

"I'm talking to you."

"Nothing. Owww!"

"Dude I really don't want to get up."

He continues to reach for the bed, ignoring me. I just watch him. He tries a few times to remove the knife but the pain is unbearable from his facial expressions.

"You're making this harder than what it has to be man." I get up and search the bed. Nothing. "There is nothing on the bed except sheets. What are you looking for?"

"Ricky! Don! Craig! Help!"

"They're dead. Oh so you must be Jack?"

"How the hell you know my name?"

"You and your gang argue very loudly. Okay so Don was missing his gun and I believe you was yelling back at him. So you still have your gun. Is that what you were looking for?"

Silence.

"You was. I may have a concussion but… but… what was I just talking about?" Wait what?

"I have daughters man!"

"Oh yeah. I forgot to check under the bed but you weren't reaching under the bed. Oh I know. Between the bed. That's where your gun is."

"Please man. Just let me live. I'll stop selling dope."

"I don't care about that. The kid cares about that. You see the kid around here? I don't." I get up to look between the mattress and box spring. "Oh shit man."

"That's my choppa man. Please man."

"If only you wore your pants properly. I'll be dead. Think about that Jack. Short for Jackson I'm guessing. Why didn't they just call you Jay?"

"Only my mom calls me tha-" He starts to whimper.

"Guess the time has come." I pick up the choppa.

Jack starts to flip the fuck out. He finally gets the strength to remove the knife. He gets up, but falls down from the blunt force of the back of the choppa hitting his head. I hit him a few more times with the gun in the back of his head until he's motionless and barely breathing. I can't shoot this guy. Not my style. Too easy. Not exciting. I turn him over. The thought of me telling Bertha that I was going to turn her and Wendy's head's into bowls of tomato soup appear in my head. I don't have a hammer but these knives will do.

I'm tired, weak, dazed, concussed. It takes some time before I enter his skull. After that it's a little easier. I chip away designing the skull bowl. Time passes and so does his life. Since his death this tomato bowl skull project hasn't been enjoyable. Silly me thinking he'll survive throughout the whole face, skull removal part. Well, now I know. The inside of your skull isn't as soupy as I thought it would be.

A few slices and dices and the project is done. Tomato soup anyone? No? Okay. I pour the soup onto the floor. That wasn't enjoyable at all. More disturbing than anything. His body wouldn't stop dancing in the beginning. It was like someone was tickling his body as I went to work on turning his head into a bowl.

Carving someone's head into a bowl of tomato soup. The

soup wasn't red enough. Chunks of bones in the soup. More brain than blood. It contains no actual tomatoes. More like a head bowl filled with the chopped up contents of someone's head. What was I thinking?

Stupid idea. You live and you learn.

I actually considered doing this to the beautiful Bertha and Wendy. I should be ashamed.

Could I be turning into a monster?

Nonsense.

I get up, leave the room, and head for the steps. Heading downstairs my head starts to thump rapidly. I hold my head in pain. Never get beat the fuck up again Donovan. I call for the kid.

No answer. Where did he go?

Fuck kid. I don't think I can make it home by myself. I yell for him.

Nothing.

Guess I'll walk myself home.

14

Where is the kid?

Dammit. I think I'm going to need help walking home. This isn't good. I don't even remember how I got to this house.

I sit next to the inground pool. I could sleep on the grass. I'm so tired and dazed. My head is painfully ringing. My head feels like it'll explode soon.

I could stay here all night but people will visit. People need their product. People need to re-up. People need their fix. Should I yell for the kid? No. The sound of yelling might kill my brain.

Oh Donovan.

Did I do this for the kid or for my pleasure? Was it even worth it Donovan?

Fuck no.

I head towards where I guess is the place where I came into this dumb situation. I'm going home. Fuck that kid. Didn't even stay to help me if I needed backup. Some hero he is.

My shirt is soaked in blood. The blood of many men. Look at you Donovan. Turning into a mass murderer. A mass murderer that nobody will acknowledge. A mass murderer that fucking sucks at his job. Is any of this a good thing or a bad thing?

My stupid fucking head won't stop throbbing.

I exit through a gate I guess I entered through earlier. It's so dark outside. This neighborhood needs more streetlights.

I guess this neighborhood doesn't have a night life. These people travel into the town or city to have fun. When you have money you can afford to.

A familiar voice calls my name.

The kid?

No. It's Mr. Worthy. Shit! I have blood all over me. What should I tell him? Should I run? What should I do Donovan? Think. My head is too fuzzy to think. Before I decide anything Mr. Worthy is right in front of me. Stupid Brain. Can't even focus when needed.

"My God. What happened?"

What the fuck do I say?

"Son. I'm speaking to you."

Talk you bitch. "The guy… guys attacked me."

"More than one? Why didn't you inform me?"

"I was jumped. When I was walking home."

"Where did all the blood come from? Where are they?"

"They ran away." I can't think. I can't think of believable bullshit to say.

"Why were you in that back yard?"

"Huh?"

"I saw you leave out that gate."

"I was just trying to find a fast way home so I can call the cops."

"You should have called me son."

"I have no cell phone." Or any energy. I feel like I'm about to faint.

"Why are you holding knives in your hand son? Where did you get them?"

I'm still holding onto the steak knives? My head is really fucked up. I drop them. I make a confused look.

"Where did they go?"

I point towards the direction of the house. Fuck. Why did I do that? I need to sit down. I sit.

The old man goes through the gate.

"I made a mistake. They went the other way. The opposite

of the way I pointed."

"Just stay here. You should have called me. I gave you my card for circumstances like this."

Fuck Donovan. Fuck, fuck, fuck, fuck.

Think you bitch. You fucked up. What do I do if he enters the house?

I must kill him.

I head into the yard. Wait Donovan. Don't forget your steak knives. I remember he has a sawed-off shotgun. What a shitty day.

Before he reaches the door to the house, an idea enters my head. The dead bodies in the pool. Thanks for finally working brain you slow processing piece of shit. I cannot allow Mr. Neighborhood Watch to see the carnage I created in that house.

"The pool Mr. Worthy. There are bodies in the pool."

"What did you say?"

"There are three dead bodies in the pool." I need to lay down.

"Oh God." Mr. Worthy utters once the rotted bodies enter his eyesight. "I think the cops will be needed. Monsters live in this neighborhood."

There aren't any monsters in this neighborhood or world. There are worst things called human beings. Men, women, and children that walk and constantly corrupt and have their wicked fun while they walk the earth. Silly Mr. Worthy.

"I must call them."

"Good. Well you have a good night Mr. Worthy. I'm headed home."

"I need you to stay. You need medical attention. You may have a concussion."

I think so too. "I must go home first."

"Then I need your number to update you."

"Sure, sure whatever. Here." I make up a number he can reach me at. I start to leave.

"You never told me why you were dual wielding knives

son. I see you picked them back up."

"It's Donovan."

"Donovan, you're not telling me everything. What happened Donovan?"

Stop asking me questions. My head is buzzing.

"The amount of blood on you is worrisome."

"I don't remember much. Just glad I'm alive."

"Go home Donovan. I need to investigate some more since your memory is apparently shot." He heads towards the house.

"No."

"Why don't you want me in that house?"

"There is nothing in that house."

"Then why is there blood on the doorknob and a trail of blood leaving the house?"

Time for you to die Mr. Worthy. I'm too tired, beaten, and weak for a head on attack so I'll wait for him to enter the house so I can stabbed him in the back. I cannot handle any form of resistance in my present state.

Cowardly?

Very.

Fortunately I don't give a shit.

A rustle in the bush a few feet to my left alert both myself and Mr. Worthy.

The kid!

Mr. Worthy sprints toward the bush. Mr. Worthy is too fast. Be smart kid. Don't do anything dumb.

Words from my mouth to no avail yell at Mr. Worthy telling him a child is in the bushes. *It's only a fucking kid.* The kid jumps out of the bushes. He says some words describing the kick he tries to defeat Mr. Worthy with.

One shotgun blast enters the kid's chest.

My heart stops.

Everything stops.

Did that just actually happen?

I grab the kid off the ground. I shake him. Wake up

kid. Stop playing around. Why would you attack someone holding a shotgun kid?

Kid?

Answer me you piece of shit. I yell at the kid. I keep shaking him. He won't wake up? Why? I notice that his chest is nonexistent. I see the blood covered grass through a hole where his chest use to belong. His cape is ruined by the shotgun blast and soaked in blood.

I place the kid back onto the grass. Kid why did you do that? What the fuck man? Where the hell were you? Were you hidden in the bushes this whole time? Why am I asking the kid these questions?

He's dead.

What the fuck kid. Tears start to roll down my face.

No.

Fuck that.

He wanted to be a little shit and play superhero then he deserved to die. I warned him numerous times. Fucking idiot. What were you doing in those bushes? I'll never know. Geez kid. A fucking hole is where your chest is supposed to be. Oh Donovan. Oh man.

Rage kills my tiredness. My head clears.

I'm awake. I'm in the present.

I snatch the shotgun from Mr. Worthy and toss it. My hands engulf his head. Words leaves his mouth but fuck what he has to say. That's not important. What's important is I'm about to snap Mr. Worthy's neck numerous times in honor of the kid. I think the kid was five years old so Mr. Worthy's neck will snap five times.

One snap in and his body is motionless. I'm not done yet you shit fuck. Sounds leave his old mouth. Second snap and he's silent. He's dead but I need three more cracks before I'm satisfied. A third and a fourth happen with some effort. I had to step on and crank his neck every which way for those breaks.

I'm having issues getting a fifth snap. His neck will break a fifth time.

HIS NECK WILL BREAK A FUCKING FIFTH TIME!

I find the shotgun. I bash his irregular neck until I hear the fifth break. It happens. I received no satisfaction. I empty the shotgun shells into his head, resulting in the disappearance of Mr. Worthy's face. Still no satisfaction. This piece of shit. I kick and stomp his genitals until they're mush. I want him even more dead but I notice a light from a house nearby and a figure looking at me through a window. I start to run away but stop for a moment to get the kid. I drag him by his leg for an instant. What the hell am I doing? There is nothing I can do for him. His heart and lungs don't exist anymore.

The kid is extinct.

I leave without the kid.

I run and I run. I have no idea where I am. Every time police lights enter my view I run the opposite way or hide in a backyard. I will not hide in a bush anywhere. I think I hate bushes now. Geez kid. I didn't even get the chance to know your real name.

Too busy playing hero together.

Through some type of magic and the planets aligning I find the sister's house. Yes. Wait. What will I say if they asked questions? It doesn't matter. They won't believe me. I smell myself. Only thing I smell is blood. Good. I'll live today.

I walk through the door to find a crying Bertha sitting on the ground right in front of the door. Like a dog waiting for their owner.

When she sees me, she screeches in horror. I must be a sight to see right now. She stands up and hugs me.

"Oh Brown Bear! What happened?"

"I need to lay down."

"Brown Bear needs a doctor Wendolynn."

"I'll call Bianca." Wendy leaves the room.

Bianca? Bianca? "Who's Bianca."

"Our friend you met. She's a registered nurse."

The faggot. No. I can't deal with this right now. I need to

lay down. "Please don't bring him."

"She's not a him Brown Bear. You will show our friend respect in this house. I know you're hurting baby but you still have some explaining to do. I'm going to allow you to rest but you will allow Bianca to patch you up then we'll have a conversation in the morning about what you've been up to." She starts to cry. "Every time we're not together you're getting into trouble. I love you Brown Bear. I won't allow this to happen again. I hate to see you in pain Brown Bear." She hugs me tighter if even possible. "I need your help Wendolynn."

We're inside Bertha's room. I lay down. I cover myself in blankets. Finally I can sleep. It's going to be hard with this headache.

"Brown Bear there is something I must do."

"Bertha I'm not in the mood for love making right now. I really need to sleep." Did I actually just refuse sex with Bertha? I must really be fucked up. I must have major head trauma.

"Oh Brown Bear. I really can't see you in pain anymore. Wendolynn get me my rope."

"Sure."

"Rope?"

"It'll be temporary Brown Bear."

"What are you talking about Bertha?"

"I'll make this as enjoyable as I can. This has to be done Brown Bear." Bertha begins to remove her clothes.

"What's happening Wendy? I just want to sleep." I had a long day.

"You'll see Donovan. It won't be so bad. Like she said it's temporary."

"I'll pin him down Wendolynn. Don't hurt my Brown Bear's wrist and ankles."

"You know I won't."

They're going to tie me up. Why? My head is too cloudy to think. Why does my head hurt?

What's happening to me?

"Okay. I won't leave the house anymore. I promise." I sound like one of my victims. I'm not sure what's going on.

Stupid head. Work Correctly.

They tell me to get naked. I comply. Bertha gets on top of me. She tries to be gentle as she pins me down. I don't fight her. She kisses me occasionally as she pins my limbs down. Her body is amazing naked. I love her body. Her breasts occasionally rub against my dick. I'm aroused. I see her beautiful pink asshole as she pins my legs down so Wendy can finish tying me up.

Why am I staring at her asshole? What the hell is going on. Why am I being tied up naked?

This woman is a goddess. I was tired five minutes ago. My head clears some but I have no idea what's going on. Did I hit my head on something? Why the fuck won't you work correctly brain?

What type of sexual adventure did these sisters manage to imagine for us tonight? I wish my head didn't hurt so much. I want to enjoy every moment of this.

The doorbell rings.

Bianca enters the room.

Shit.

I don't want to enjoy this shit.

How did I forget? What the fuck brain. How could you forget something so important? My blood boils. His smug look pisses me off. I'm beyond pissed. I feel defeated. Bianca the female imposter has seen me naked and I allowed the beautiful, naked Bertha to distract me.

I'm an idiot.

"Hey Brown Bear." Bianca speaks with his fake womanly voice. It's a terrible voice. You're not fooling anyone in this room.

"Don't you dare call me that."

"You're no fun."

"Don't you dare touch my dick." I gnaw my teeth at him.

I'm a trapped animal. I've been set up. How could Bertha do this to me.

"Oh I won't darling. I know you belong to Bertha. You can't stop me from kissing you."

He blows me a kiss.

I dodge it.

"I'll bite your fucking lips off."

"Be nice Brown Bear." Bertha says as she slaps my balls a little too hard. "You'll do no such thing to our friend. Now be nice."

"This is very uncomfortable I must say." I struggle trying to free myself but the thumping pain in my head stops my escape attempt.

I fucking hate you brain. I can't believe I fucking forgot he was coming over. I'm tied up, naked in front of him.

"Brown Bear, relax. You need medical attention."

I sigh. "Okay Bertha." I turn to Bianca. "Just know if you do something I don't like, you'll pay for it."

"Trust me Donovan. I won't bite."

You better fucking not you piece of tranny dirt shit.

15

Three stitches above my right eye. Two black eyes. Right side of my jaw swollen. A concussion to top it off. I got fucked up. I'm alive though. Can't say the same about Mr. Rock Fist at that drug house.

It's been days, maybe a week and some change and I'm still tied up. I don't know. I lost track of the days. I think there are trust issues in our relationship. Girlfriends don't tie up their boyfriends when they don't trust them. Bertha isn't any girlfriend though. She's the girlfriend of all girlfriends. Crazy to the power of crazy. Oh man. I wonder what she'll think if I ever referred to her as my girlfriend. Bertha would most likely be offended thinking we're already married in that mind of hers.

Women.

Relationships.

Bertha and I had our talk about why I was gone that night. She was naked during the whole conversation except for a lace purple thong. She's angry at me. I cannot take her seriously when her tits are smiling right at me. I just wanna make love to that woman. I doubt I made eye contact the whole time we talked.

As always she doesn't believe me. Threats were thrown my direction. Balls were handled roughly during Bertha's lecturing. It was kind of a turn on. She didn't like that so she squeezed until I didn't enjoy the situation, continuing her threats. My explanation pissed her off. The blood all over me as proof wasn't enough to release me.

So I apologized and apologized. Again and again. Told her I would never cheat on someone as beautiful as her. Somehow that worked and she was happy and forgiving.

I survived.

It hasn't been too bad staying in a bed for however long I've been in this bed. There is no TV in the room. No laptop. No porn. No problem. My penis is pleased often. Balls are played with. I'm pleased. Bertha is pleased. Even Wendy.

Those ladies are Heaven sent. It feels good having all the work done unto you. I just lay tied up on my back. All I need is a hard dick.

Check.

Bertha has been going into overtime though after I cum on multiple occasions. I can't defend myself. I'm defenselessly tied up. I almost blacked out from pleasure because she wouldn't stop bouncing or sucking on my dick after climax. That woman. She's so unnaturally stunning. I don't think I'll ever want natural again. Except Wendy.

Bianca was surprisingly respectful during our unfortunate encounter the first night of my imprisonment. He said one sly remark though. Said he could see my pretty brown asshole. Such a faggot. Still can't believe he saw me naked.

He stayed the night after patching me up in case there were complications. Why would there be any? I only got beat the fuck up. You don't know how to do your job properly? I think he likes me. He wanted to stay in the room that night. Yeah okay guy. Get the fuck outta here.

Bianca tried bathing me. Fuck that. I made Wendy and Bertha do that. Why do I keep calling him Bianca? I gotta find out his real name. Probably an Andre or something. Terrell maybe.

The sisters have been doing an amazing job bathing me. It's been very sexual. I almost came a few times because they take a half an hour to washed my private parts. The bed gets soaked because they refused to allow me to leave the bed to take a real bath.

I get washed with a rag with hand soap squeezed on it while I'm tied up on the bed. I'm stuck lying on the bed cold after and then a fan freezes my naked body trying to dry the bed and me. For some reason they won't dry me off with a towel. There are plenty of towels in this fucking house. I doubt these sisters are the brightest in the world. Maybe the most exotic but definitely not the brightest. I'll take exotic.

Bertha said she's going to buy a new bed for us. I hope so because soon this bed will be moldy as shit.

Using the bathroom has been and continues to be tough. Bertha or Wendy won't allow me to leave the bed to relieve myself. My pecker is held and pointed in the direction of a bucket when I have to piss.

I can't stop getting hard when they touch me. Then I either can't piss or go through the agony of pissing with a boner. The first few times I pissed on the bed because they didn't bring the bucket close enough.

Shitting is another story. I'm tied to the edge of the bed in a way that my ass is hanging over the bed so I can shit in a bucket half filled with water. This is inhumane. Why don't the sisters tie me in a similar position so I can pee properly instead of trying to pee while I'm lying on my back?

The world will never know.

It's the weirdest feeling having someone else wipe your ass. I feel so violated. I feel pathetic. They don't even trust me to wipe my own shitty ass. Where is the trust. I think about shitting myself so they're forced to take me off this bed. I could use a vacation from being tied up on a wet, soon to be moldy bed. My little revenge for the sisters using a fan to dry me off. I haven't had the courage to shit myself.

I've been getting fed well. First they were making me sandwiches but I stopped that after a few days. Sadly their sandwich making skills are subpar. Such a disappointment. That realization was borderline tear jerking. The sandwich Goddesses must be ashamed. Twice they forgot to feed me. They blamed me for not reminding them. I'm the one tied up. I'm the prisoner.

Women.

About two days after Bianca patched me up and my head cleared up, I woke up and my asshole was wet with what I can only guess was shit. Diarrhea. Fuck! I shit myself. I must have thought of shitting myself into existence.

What will they think?

Donovan shit himself. Brown Bear shit himself.

I was wrong. It wasn't shit. I found out it was lube.

Either Bertha or Wendy lubed up my asshole while I slept. They wouldn't tell me the guilty party. Next thing I know, the ladies walked into the room with the skimpiest lingerie I ever saw them wear. My dick is instantly hard from the sight of them. One of Wendy's nipples are out. Bertha's ass is oiled up and as big and beautiful as ever. Oh man.

Yes!

Contained in each of their hands are three dildos of varying sizes and various anal beads. What the fuck are y'all thinking about?

Bertha feels bad I've been in this bed for a few days and wishes to make it up to me with the help of Wendy. What the hell is going through your mind Bertha? What kinky shit have you thought up this time? I explain to them that I'll love to use those toys on them but they'll need to untie me first.

Wendy starts to laugh. Bertha has a concerned look on her face. Bertha wants to be a little kinky today and allow those toys to explore my asshole. I politely tell her no thank you but thanks for the offer. Fuck that.

Bertha doesn't like my answer. She starts to play with my hard dick telling me how much she enjoys anal play and how much I'll like it. Wendy tries to convince me also, giggling throughout her persuasion. Bertha hits Wendy for not acting serious because this is serious. You can tell in her eyes. Bertha tells me how Bianca's partners love it.

Because they're gay.

Also, mentioning sex and Bianca in the same sentence is a major turn off. I'm surprised my dick stayed rock hard. The sight of these women. Then she tells me that she'll be gentle and will buy me whatever I want after.

Really Bertha? You trying to negotiate sticking something up my ass? I politely tell them that the only thing I like in my ass is shit. Wendy basically falls on the floor laughing. I'm glad you find this funny Wendy. Bertha concedes and gives me a blowjob, finally smiling and looking happy once I cum. She tells me maybe next time. Yeah okay.

I love Bertha.

The kid. I've been thinking about him. I don't miss him. He was okay to have around even though he forced our encounters. Kinda annoying too. Why did you have to be so nosey kid?

What the hell was his name? He had to tell me. Epic something? No Donovan. That was his superhero name. Dammit.

Well the kid did allow me to kill a few people so I give him that. Five kills in one night. Thanks kid. You were good for something. I kinda do miss you now. Thinking about it if you were still here you'll probably find a way into this room because you don't respect privacy. You could have been my way out of this prison kid. Why did you have to die days ago?

Well I guess he died doing what he loved if pretending to be a superhero and fighting crime is worth dying over. I want to miss him but I can't find that thing that people use when they miss someone. I think it's called emotions or caring or something. I don't know. If I had a manual on finding emotions I probably could find it inside myself. Is it like a switch you turn on in your brain? I wonder if you could buy it.

I didn't notice it before but when these ladies leave the house they're gone for hours or what I'm guessing is hours. There is no clock in Bertha's room. Thanks Bertha. I know

Wendy has a job but what does Bertha do? I never asked.

They leave for hours, come back, and then leave for hours again even at night. I'm not getting lonely. I'm just erect the majority of the time, tied up, alone, with no way of releasing the pressure between my legs. Even at night when Bertha surprisingly sleeps next to me on this wet bed, she sometimes leaves in the middle of the night.

What the hell?

Is she cheating on me? Am I jealous?

She wouldn't. She too is against cheating. Murdered people for it.

Stupid emotions. They appear when I don't want them too. Work when I want you to work.

She must really love me sleeping on this cold, fucking wet bed next to me. She could just sleep with her sister is she wanted to. You don't have to torture yourself too. I do like the company while I'm in prison though. I don't like how my wrist and ankles are getting burned and scarred by this fucking rope.

I have to stop trying to escape.

Accept your punishment.

There has been a bug crawling on me for the last hour. I don't know what type of bug it is but it has bit me a few times. Stupid bug. This bug keeps crawling near my balls.

This bitch bug made it to my balls.

You better not bite my fucking balls you bug. The bug has bitten me a few times near my balls on my thigh. These bites are starting to itch. Get off my balls you bitch bug. I wiggle him back onto my leg.

A door opens. The front door.

Yes! Someone is home.

Damn I'm excited. Someone get this bug off me and turn this fan off. I'm cold.

"Hello my beautiful naked Brown Bear!"

Very descriptive. Why is she smiling so hard? "Hey Bertha."

"I got you a present." She's wearing a tight, bright pink dress. Her boobs are practically bursting from the dress.

Nice present. "I love the new dress. You didn't have to buy that for me to see you in. I like you naked."

"No Brown Bear. This." She raises the box wrapped in red wrapping paper in her hand.

Oh. "Oh. Thanks."

"Always the funny guy. Now close your eyes."

"Okay."

"Don't peek."

"Okay."

"I mean it Brown Bear."

"Okay."

Tits rub against my face. This is turning out as a lovely present. Wait a second. Why is she being so nice? What is in that box? Where did that fucking bug go? "You got something for my butt in that box?"

"No Brown Bear. Unfortunately I do not. Now be quiet."

I hear wrapping paper ripped apart. The box is opened.

"Open your eyes."

I do.

"Surprise!"

A watch?

"You like it?"

A watch.

"Do you like it?"

She's smiling this hard and this excited over a watch?

"You're not saying anything Brown Bear."

"I love it." It's a watch.

"Really?"

"Yes." It's a basic digital watch.

"I knew you would. Put it on." She hands the watch to me.

"Can't. I'm currently tied up. Did you forget? And I don't think my wrist would like to wear a watch right now. My wrist are in terrible condition Bertha."

"Oh right. I'll untie it. Your wrist will be fine. I'll kiss them later." She unties my right hand and puts the watch on rather forcefully. "I have another surprise. You're free. I'm not going to keep my Brown Bear tied up anymore. I need to have more trust in this relationship. I trust you Brown Bear."

Geez thanks Bertha. "Glad there is trust. It's important."

"Please Brown Bear. Don't make me kill you."

"Sure. Why would I ever want that." This is one crazy relationship.

"I love you Brown Bear."

"Love you too."

"Would you like a treat before I set you free?"

"I wasn't free before?"

"Do you want a treat or not?"

I do.

16

I'm sitting on a wooden bench at a park. It's what people consider a beautiful day outside. No clouds. No rain. Great sunshine. Smooth wind. Relaxing. What I consider beautiful is seeing Bertha and Wendy naked while there's a thunder storm outside. Beautiful assets over nature any day.

Also if the day contains ending a life. Gets the red juices flowing. Being in control of life or death makes the heart pump more life into you.

That control makes you more alive than you ever were.

My kind of beautiful day.

I guess it is nice out. A few milfs with their children. Mostly blondes. Nice butts. Tight jeans. Short skirts. Large fake breasts. If there weren't any children around I could crank one out quick.

Too risky.

Can't afford jail time. Can't afford being caught. Wouldn't that be great. Of all the things I go to jail for, it's for beating my dick in front of a dozen kids. I will not unhave this erection though. Quality eye candy in front of me. Wish I know about this park earlier.

It's a good thing I will not masturbate here. Next time my balls are in Bertha's mouth she'll notice they're smaller than when I left earlier and my penis smells a little too funky. Next thing I know Bertha is measuring my balls with some caliper that she happened to have and *BOOM!*

I'm dead.

I can't win with this woman.

This one milf catches my eye. She's thick.
Check.
Has a sexy accent.
Check.
Fat ass.
Check.
Nice boobs.
Check.
She's playing soccer with what I guess are her two children. You could never tell she was once pregnant. No loose skin. Flat stomach. Surgery after? I don't know.

Her dress keeps rising up. Her pale ass and black thong excite me. Why do these kids have to be here. Dammit. Maybe if I wiggle a certain way while looking at her ass dance while she playfully plays soccer, I'll have the private release I want. What the hell Donovan. What if someone sees me. I'll look like an idiot wiggling on this wooden bench.

Fuck.

I decide to stop looking at the beautiful sights around me for fear I may wiggle out an orgasm in my pants and live my last moments getting my balls measured and a gun to my head. Can't believe I'm going to avoid these images in front of me.

Stupid kids.

Stupid Bertha's insecurities.

I hate you all.

I see these three kids playing basketball with their father or uncle I'm guessing. Sounds weird saying father. Father. What the fuck is a father? Would a father have made my life different? The world will never know. I like how I turned out.

He has two daughters and a son. His son appears the youngest and is garbage at playing basketball. He can't even shoot the basketball near the hoop. He's looks like he's five or six but still the ball needs to go into the basket little kid. I continue to watch them play, the two daughters scoring the majority of their baskets with the father making his and the little child traveling with the ball and throwing the basketball up in the air.

What the hell kid.

You call that a layup?

This cannot be basketball this kid is playing. He's just happy to be on the court. Get off the court you bum I want to yell. I'm not the greatest basketball player but this kid is light years away from where I'm at. Find another sport kiddo.

They continue to play. The one sister drives to her left by her brother. He trips on his shoe. What a bum. I continue to watch. I want to observe these milfs around me though but I also want to live.

Dammit Bertha.

Why do you torment you even when you're away?

Something amazing happens. The kid actually makes a basket. Oh shit. About time you bum. You might actually make your dad proud someday.

For some odd reason I continue to watch this guy play basketball with his children instead of appreciating the sight of milfs prancing around the park.

Oh my god Donovan. You're crazy. I still take my occasional looks.

The one daughter trips. Her shoestring gets caught under her opposite shoe. A hard crash onto the concrete is avoided with the girl bracing her fall with her hands. Stupid girl. Tie your shoe. No cry or yell of pain leaves her mouth. This girl is tough. She gets up to tie her shoe. How is she not crying? I know she banged her hands hard. They have to be pretty bruised. One tough little girl. I look away from her for a moment and my eyes meets the dad's eyes. I quickly look away.

The dad approaches me. What the hell does he want? I can't watch a family play terrible basketball?

The dad has a serious look on his face. He has a douchey military haircut. Army veteran maybe. What do you want Mister?

"Can I ask what you're doing at the park today?"

"Enjoying this beautiful day."

"And that involves watching me and my children play basketball?"

"I'm not allowed to watch?"

"You can do whatever the fuck you want. Why were you staring at my daughter's ass when she fell on the ground?"

What the fuck is he talking about?

That statement startles me. She fell. I looked. The end. "Excuse me?"

"And why the hell is your hand grabbing your dick?"

I look down at my hand.

Fuck.

His tone of voice becomes more serious. "Sir let me see some ID."

"What is going on? Did I do something wrong?" My heart starts to race.

Why the fuck is my hand touching my dick? Why are you still hard?

Shit Donovan.

I must have been touching myself, unbeknown to myself, while admiring the ladies around the park.

Fuck.

How long have you been touching him Handrea?

"You're actions are alarming. I need to see some form of identification. I'm not going to ask again."

"Daddy is everything ok?" The son asks, running up to their dad while his older sisters tag along.

"Get back Billy. Go back and play basketball with your sisters."

The son leaves with the two sisters. The dad's full attention is back to me.

"I'm going to ask you one last time kid or I'm going to call my guys down at the station. Show me some fucking ID."

"Are you a cop?"

"Yes."

Fucking pig harassing me at the park. "Where is your badge?"

"I don't got fucking time for this." He pulls out his phone.

"Okay. Stop. I don't have ID on me. My name is Donovan Burgundy"

"You better not be lying to me boy." He starts dialing numbers.

"I have nothing to hide." Shit I gotta get out of here.

Run?

No.

Snap his neck?

No.

Too many witnesses around.

I look around while the dad waits for an answer on the other line. I count at least five families close enough to see or hear any harm I can inflict on this annoying pig. How am I going to get out of this? Why did I have to be alone at a park looking at parents play with their kids. Why did I even come to a park today?

"Fuck. My phone died. What's your address?"

"I think my name is enough."

I'm getting out of here.

My shoulder is grabbed.

"You have what you need. I'm leaving. Go play with your kids."

He curses some threats. I leave the park.

I'm sweating. That could have turned out different. I was actually enjoying my park visit too. Enough of the park for me today. Stupid fucking pig cop. One guy cannot enjoy his visit to the park? He thought I was being a pedophile fondling myself to his children playing.

Fuck that guy.

Fuck pedophiles.

I'm on a random street a few blocks from the park. What should Donovan do next? I could use some well needed sexual pleasure from the one and only Bertha. Sounds good to me. Now if only I knew how to get back home.

This isn't good.

I try one street and then another, hoping some detail on some street ignites some memory in my head that reminds myself how to get home. I thought I've been on every street this town had to offer. Guess not. Wait a second. None of this looks familiar. I've never walked around here.

The people look unfamiliar. These kids playing in their driveways are new. What the hell? Dammit. I left the park on the opposite side that I entered. Now I gotta find my way back to the park. Can't believe that cop guy got me this distracted. You gotta be smarter Donovan. You did nothing wrong so you have nothing to worry about.

The park is found. Congrats Donovan. You've done something correct today. That cop is still playing basketball with his kids. I can either go through the park to get to the street I need or around the park. I choose around. Don't feel like getting harassed a second time. I should though. It's faster. This is America. I should be able to walk through a park anytime without being harassed.

Just walk around Donovan.

There is pleasure waiting for you at home.

As I'm walking around the park, I notice more grade A milfs have entered for some outside activities with their kids. Am I really going to walk home because some off duty cop thinks I'm a pervert and miss out on what's available and bouncing and enhanced right in front of my face?

Think Donovan.

You got that lady over there. Definitely D cups in the peach dress. Borderline double D's. Plus she has a round, toned ass. Am I really going to go home and miss that? How many times will you see that again? But I have Bertha plus Wendy at home and none of these women are in the same class as them. Not even the same category. Dammit. But this is a good appetizer before the meal. But unfortunately this appetizer won't be enjoyed because that cop is looking my way.

He's holding the basketball while he stares me down from the other side of the park. What the hell man. I'm nowhere near you or your kids. Keep playing basketball. Yeah look at me all you want you piece of shit. Nobody is worried about your fucking piglets. I can't walk around the park? You gotta problem with that too? He continues to stare at me. Yeah my appetizer is ruined.

Fuck that guy.

I head home.

I make it home and I'm greeted with two sisters arguing at each other. That's new.

Curses are thrown across the room. A few curses in one sentence from Wendy. A few more from another sentence from Bertha and vice versa. What are they arguing about?

Bertha sadly is covered in a flower printed beach towel. Nothing for me to admire is revealed. Fucking beach towel. Her hair is wet. No makeup is hiding her true appearance. If I would have came home sooner I would've had a sight to see. A body of a goddess wet from head to toe. Dammit Donovan. Fucking stupid cop distracted me and made me waste time.

Wendy is wearing a neon orange tank top and black leggings. A matching neon orange thong can be seen under the leggings. Her cleavage is overly revealed. How are those two breasts not popping out of her shirt? I'm instantly hard, betting they'll fall out very soon. Seconds soon hopefully. I'm praying she'll motion a certain way to free them so my eyes may be treated to their sight. A guy can hope. Wendy's hair is done and makeup is covering her natural beauty.

They continue and continue to go back and forth arguing. Their voices grow louder. Their faces redder. My erection harder. The thought of these two women this angry while we have sex excites me. Excites me a little too much I must admit. I want the sisters to have angry sex with me now. I approach Bertha to get her attention. She hasn't acknowledged me once since I came into the house. Wendy either for that matter.

This is new.

I rub on her beach towel covered breasts.

No response.

I caress her large butt.

Nothing.

I lift the towel up to touch her naked butt. That always works.

I'm pushed away.

The hell?

I go to take the towel off. My hands are grabbed and removed from the beach towel by Bertha. "Now is not the time Brown Bear." Bertha explains to me with beyond serious eyes looking directly into mine own.

I've never seen her look like this.

I turn to Wendy.

"Go somewhere and play Donovan. Bertha and I are having a conversation."

They return to yelling at each other.

Go play? Am I a kid to them or something. *Go play Donovan. Bertha and I are having a conversation. Now is not the time Brown Bear.* What the hell is going on with these two? What the hell happened when I left? I've been gone for about… I check the watch Bertha gave me… two, three hours max.

If only I didn't walk home the wrong way to start I would have some idea of what they're voicing their loud opinions about back and forth to each other. I try to make sense of it. Lies were told. Lies weren't told. Trust issues. There aren't trust issues. More stuff is yelled I can't make sense of.

Wendy's cleavage is a huge distraction. She isn't even wearing a bra. I didn't notice the luscious nipples pressing against her neon orange tank top earlier. Dammit! When will they stop arguing! They're females so there may never be an end to it. I leave the room and head for the kitchen to make myself a sandwich, looking in the living room occasionally hoping an article of clothing doesn't do its job and I'm blessed to see a big, juicy womanly accessory.

It'll be amazing if they fought. Something will definitely pop out.

Fingers crossed.

It's getting dark outside. I'm sitting on the couch in the living room. Each sister is in her room with their doors locked. It has to be some petty sister drama they were arguing about. Probably arguing over stealing and wearing each other clothes. Makes sense. Unfortunately for me I don't have a key to either room and I believe from earlier it'll be safer if I stay out of their paths. No knocking will be coming from me on their doors. Still can't believe they essentially brushed me off earlier like I was dust on their shirt.

Women.

What to do Donovan? What to do. I could masturbate but I rather not waste an orgasm in case one of the sisters happen to open one of these doors tonight. They both have to be horny. Bertha and Wendy cannot go a few hours without pleasure. They must be fiending for it by now. That also could explain their anger.

Horny for their one and only Donovan. They couldn't decide who would have me first so they engaged in a shouting battle. Yeah, that's what happened. Well we all lost because none of us are getting any. The image of them naked and wet between their legs begging for my services makes me grow hard.

I need sex. Dammit. I need it. Why did I have to imagine them naked. Oh Donovan. I need it. Should I knock on their door? It can't hurt. The worst that could happened is a no from both sisters. That's better than never even asking. Fingers and toes crossed.

I approach Wendy's door first. She's calmer and less wild than Bertha. I have a better chance of some pleasure by knocking on her door. Plus I didn't appreciate the way Bertha brushed me off. I thought I was your Brown Bear?

A weird sound is coming from Wendy's room. Moaning? No. Sounds like her cell phone is vibrating rather loudly. What's that sound? Dammit Donovan. She's using a vibrator and that is moaning. Fuck. You rather have a sex toy than have me tonight Wendy?

Fuck that toy. All it can do is vibrate and vibrate. Stupid sex toy.

Bertha's room is next. Going to Wendy's room was a waste of my precious time. I hear moans but no vibrations. What the fuck is going on! Am I becoming obsolete to these women? I become pissed. I grow hot. I bang on her door. A few seconds pass and the door opens. I'm greeted with a naked Bertha glistening in sweat. Oh my god I want this woman right now. I grow harder.

"What?"

I wasn't expecting that for a hello.

"Ummm…" What the hell do I say? Think. This isn't turning out how I imagined. Why is she so pissed? "I was wondering if you could use Brown Bear's company?" I smile at her. Did I just fucking call myself Brown Bear?

I'm pathetic. I'm horny and pathetic.

"No. Is that all you wanted?"

I look at her hand that isn't holding the door open. That fucking, stupid, piece of shit, long, big black fucking dildo is clutched in her hand and lathered in her wetness. I try not to growl at it. That piece of shit.

Relax Donovan. It's just a dildo.

She rather have an inanimate object fucking her pussy and asshole than me? She rather make love to a dildo? Sadness overwhelms me. I'm defeated. The big black dildo has won the night.

"Sorry to bother you," is all I can reply to her. The door

is swiftly slammed in my face and my erection vanishes. Moans instantly sing from Bertha's room. Is she fucking herself standing up, right behind the door, inches from me? All I can do is shake my head.

I leave the house.

It's nighttime. I'm headed back to the park. I don't know why but I am. I have nowhere else to go but I'm definitely not staying in a house when the sisters will be using everything in here other than myself to pleasure themselves.

Fuck that.

I walk in darkness to the park. Not many people walk around in this neighborhood at night. A few people walking their little expensive dogs but that's about it. It's a nice neighborhood. You'll see more people walk around in a dirty, rotten, violent neighborhood than a calm and peaceful one. I guess when you don't have shit in the house, you search for it outside.

The park at night is well illuminated. Like a fancy restaurant at night when all the lights are dimmed. The courts are visible enough to partake in some games after sunset. All the park equipment is visible enough to still be used at night. Why don't they do this at every park? I head over to the swings.

I don't remember the last time I was on a swing set. I remember they were my favorite activity at the park. Now it's looking at milfs prance around the park with their children. You cannot stay young forever. You grow up and your tastes change. I still remember how to swing. Don't swing too high Donovan. I don't think these are for adults to swing on.

I swing and I swing. Today I've seen so many beautiful woman and all I have from those sights are erections that didn't get any action. Not even hand action. I should have just watched porn tonight.

No you shouldn't.

You're better than that. You evolved Donovan. No more

beating your dick in front of a computer screen. You fuck vaginas and assholes and mouths now. You make love to women. Sometimes you fuck women. You don't fuck your own hand anymore.

You don't fuck Handrea anymore.

She got you in trouble today.

You make love to beautiful women now. Real women. Remember that. Watching porn is so easy though. Go on the billions of free sites and masturbate to whatever unique category gets your dick the hardest. The hours I wasted making love to my hands while images of imitation lovemaking ruined my brain. Porn can't even touch the real thing. Wish I found out sooner.

I notice a lady sitting on a park bench with a baby a good distance away from me while swinging. She pulls both her breasts out. I hop off the swing. Oh shit. Is she about to breastfeed her baby? I sneak over, crawling occasionally to a tree near the lady with a great view of her rack. Her breasts are huge. Her breasts are lovely and pale. Nipples are cute and pink.

The baby is lying next to her on the bench, covered in light blue blankets. I'm a good distance away from her. I'm hidden in the darkness of the night. No lights are around me to ruin my location. If the lady looks towards my direction, all she's see is the night. My penis is erect. I pull him out of my pants. Am I really about to do this? I haven't beaten off in so long. Her breasts look so lovely though. I think this is the best action I'll get tonight. Hand action with a view I doubt I'll see again. At least this in better than sitting in a dark room all alone hammering away for hours on end.

I start jacking him.

Minutes pass. I'm astonished by her breasts. I don't know if it's the situation I'm in jerking off behind a tree while looking at some huge boobs at a park at night but this is exhilarating. My penis feels harder and harder in my hands. I feel like I will cum soon. The lady picks her baby up and the baby latches onto her left breast. I continue masturbating for a few seconds but the sight of this baby sucking mommy's boob is kind of a major buzzkill. I let go of my penis. He becomes soft. Does this count as child porn? Please God don't let it count. Was I really just masturbating behind a tree while looking at a lady's breasts before she breastfeeds her child?

Yes you were Donovan.

My life is falling apart.

I've hit a new low.

I just stare at the breast that is not nurturing the baby. I relax and lie against the tree. I'm tapped on my shoulder. A voice that sounds very familiar speaks to me.

"Perverts never learn."

It's that dad cop. I face him.

"Put your dick back in your pants. Absolutely pathetic."

I obliged. My stomach churns. Is this embarrassment I'm feeling?

Yes it is you fucking idiot.

I think I'm going to be sick. I just got caught masturbating to a mother breastfeeding her child. My cheeks increase in temperature. I'm lost for words. I want to run but my legs won't do anything else but shake. Run Donovan. Run.

"Put these on."

Handcuffs? Am I being arrested? My mind clears. Why is he wearing all black with gloves in the summertime? I notice he's wearing a cotton hat. Ski mask maybe?

Run Donovan.

I run.

I'm tripped by the pig. His weight overpowers me. I struggle and fight to get up. My face is slammed in the dirt. My right arm is cranked in an awkward position. I yell in pain. I hear the mother scream from a distance and run off with her baby, shoes smacking against the concrete. The pig informs me that he likes when they fight. Gets his heart racing. He enjoys the rush.

The fuck is up with this guy?

I'm handcuffed. Something is thrown over my head. All I see is darkness. I'm forced to my feet. I'm told if I do anything to remove what's over my head this will happen: I'm kicked in my nuts. My stomach goes sour. I fall to my knees. I call the cop a bitch. Another kick in the nuts. I fight back losing everything that's in my stomach.

Something blunt strikes me on the left side of my face. A few kicks to my ribs. Groans leave my mouth. I start to panic. I'm forced to my feet and told to shut the fuck up. I'm hunched over. My side is in so much pain. I'm pushed forward and told to keep walking.

I'm told to stop. A car door opens. I'm shoved inside. My heart is pounding in my throat.

Time passes. It's hard to tell how much. A few stops happen. Violent stops. I'm thrown around the back seat with each stop, my face and shoulders taking a beating each time.

A door opens. I'm dragged out of the car by my shirt. I'm thrown onto hard concrete. It's hard to breath with this thing covering my head. Hands slap my face multiple times. I'm told to get on my knees and don't move. I plead not to suck his dick. Another crotch kick. I think I might piss myself.

The cop tells me to stop moving. Some type of string is tied around my neck. It's even harder to breath with this thing over my head. I'm panicking. Heart pounding in numerous areas in my body. That's all I can hear. Relax Donovan. Slow your breathing down you bitch.

I'm scared.

"In a perfect world you'll be dead by now you fucking disgusting pedophile. In a not so perfect world you'll be in jail getting brutally beaten day in and day out. Being a pedophile is a sickness. Unfortunately in my world I remove what causes that sickness."

"*NO!*"

"I said shut up!" More kicks to the crotch and slaps to the face.

I don't shut up.

I'm no pedophile.

I need my dick.

Oh God help me.

Someone please help me.

I scream for help. I try to chew the cover off my face. I'm borderline waterboarding myself with my sweat soaked in this cloth covering my head.

His foot connects with my jaw, dazing me. Fists pound my face. I'm told to get up. I can't. Fear of my end paralyses me.

"Where the *FUCK* are my gloves? Shit! I left them in the house. Shit! You are one lucky motherfucker tonight. I'm not touching your dick bare handed. *Fuck!* But what I will do is beat the living shit out of you. I better never see you ever again you fucking sick piece of shit."

I say nothing.

Something thick and solid smashes into my face. Then my leg. Then my stomach, ribs, and face.

It breaks.

The sound of satisfaction leaves his mouth. I struggle to groan.

I wish I was already dead.

He palms my head and proceeds to smash it into the concrete again and again and again and again and aga-

17

Is it worse to be in pain or to be dead? Pain brings suffering. Death brings death. Pain allows a chance for redemption. Healing. Adaptation. Death gives nothing except an end to pain. I think about the two as I lie on concrete.

Pain is a horrible truth. Medicine can only hide it. Pain will soon reveal itself. It controls your mind. Tells you something is wrong. Makes your body foreign. Nothing works correctly. You can't turn it off. It's a non-stop virus. Disease. You can't be normal again.

Take more medicine and now it becomes pain. Pain stays pain. Medication becomes pain. Peace is pain. You can't control you. Now I see why so many people kill themselves. Life is painful.

Pain is painful.

Tried moving about an hour ago. Body ignited in torture, head screamed to end the suffering. You turn into someone else when pain enters you. You start to believe death is not such a bad idea. Death turns into a craving.

I'm starting to crave death.

Movement became my enemy. Death is a needed ally.

Save me Death.

I can only see out of one eye. Barely. I'm not broken but in pain. Serious pain. The worst pain is the pain you can't control. I can't control this. I didn't choose this. I can choose death. Die Donovan.

I can control pain. Not now. Later. Choose pain or death Donovan.

I choose pain. Death doesn't allow revenge. I need it. Revenge. Death is a cruel bitch. Fuck Death. I need someone else to enjoy this pain. At least try to.

I try to enjoy it.

Brain cannot bear this pain. Brain won't allow me to move. I've lost control of myself. Pain has won.

No.

Can pain become a friend? Must get friendly with this pain. Then maybe I could get acquainted with another pain. Movement. Movement has become pain. Pain is a terrifying friend.

Someone walks in the distance.

Yes.

Hope.

Yell Donovan.

No. That'll be a new pain.

Pain is starting to become a bitch like death. I slowly circle my jaw. Pain introduces itself. We've met already. No rattling of bones. I can yell if I want. Are you ready to meet pain again Donovan?

I yell.

Pain.

Yes and hope also. A person approaches. A lady. I won. Fuck pain.

No I haven't.

I'm rolled over.

Pain.

Will it end?

I'm asked questions. I answer each question in my head. Pain is winning. I'm losing. Speak Donovan.

Question after question after question. I answer in a way she cannot understand. She looks concerned. Now she's in pain. I notice her breasts.

They're big. Round. I can barely see them. Can't touch them. Pain prevents me from enjoying something I love. Death almost made breasts nonexistent.

I hate death.

I hate pain. Pain's power is frightening.

I can win. Accept defeat Donovan.

I speak. I answer questions. I lose. Pain wins.

No.

I win. I'm caressed. I'm helped by a beautiful women. Breasts give me hope. Breasts rub against me. Yes. Pain still kinda wins. I can't fully enjoy this. Let's call it a tie. But I remember something. I can control pain. Especially on others.

Donovan you fucking idiot. How could you forget? Pain brings you joy. Pain is powerful. Pain can bring pain or joy. I choose joy. Fuck pain also. This fucking hurts. I'm going to share pain. I must heal first.

I give the kind lady a painful hug. Painful for me. I miss breasts. I like how they feel pressed against my chest. I miss Bertha and Wendy. I miss their breasts. I tell the lady to take me home. No hospital. I said no hospital lady. Dammit. Bertha will not be happy. Pain. It won't end but it will.

It is difficult to stop a woman that loves you from hurting another woman that only helped when you look the way I do.

Bertha is pissed.

How dare you take my job and be his savior when I should have been there. How dare you console him before I do. I should have been there for my Brown Bear, not you. Why the fuck are you crying? That's not your Brown Bear. He's my Brown Bear. I should be crying you crooked tit bitch, not you. My love and care should have fondled him first.

Pain prevents me from stopping Bertha from pounding this woman in front of the house. I'm lying against the front door. My legs are weak. The lady is lying against the stone walk way. Unconscious. She's then thrown into Bertha's car.

It's early in the morning. No witnesses except me. Bertha carefully takes me into her home. I beg not to be punished.

She promises not to. I try to cross my fingers. I hope I didn't break anything. I'm asked to tell her what happened. I ask where Wendy is. Bertha's face changes. Potential pain refocuses me. I tell her only what needs to be told. I got beat the fuck up at a park late at night. I describe to her in many words what happened. I'm stripped and my manhood is gently caressed. Is that the only part of the story she cares about? Everything on me hurts Bertha.

She knows.

Somehow I'm hard. My testicles ache.

She knows.

No sex.

Thank you Bertha.

Bertha cleans me up a little. Bianca comes sometime later. He mends my wounds. Thanks? He has seen me naked once again. I have to stop losing. Stop hesitating. Unleash Donovan. Remember pain is good on others. Not yourself. I should literally get that drilled into my mind.

Bertha takes a nap next to me in bed. She's wearing a nightgown. She's a little mad at me. I'm putting her through a lot of pain. I shouldn't cause her pain. My pain destroys Bertha. She looked like a sad puppy when Bianca was stitching me back together. Her Brown Bear is broken. She's upset. Bertha knows I like to see her sleep naked. I will avenge our pain Bertha. I must heal first.

Days go by. Healing is a slow process. Time to think.

Think Donovan. Think.

I know what to do.

I think and I plan. Bertha continues to sleep in a nightgown. I plan. I will fix this Bertha.

I'm questioned about the watch she has given me for a gift. I lost it. I didn't notice it was gone. Why does it matter, I think. It must have got broken or stolen when I received my beating at the park. She gives me another one. Same watch. Okay? Wendy needs to give Bertha a lesson in gifts.

I only look at her hands when she's sleeping. I'm too

afraid to look when she's conscious. I'm surprised she doesn't put on gloves when she leaves the house. I know people stare at her hands. Bertha must proudly show them as a warning. Fuck with me and I'll do everything possible to make sure you don't live anymore. I sleep next to crazy.

Her hands are not a turn off but they're definitely not a turn on. She'll never have a career in hand modeling. She killed that career when she used her hands as duct tape to keep lye from leaving one of her exes' mouths. I don't remember his name. He's dead. I'm not. I'm just glad she has other things to crave and admire other than her chewed up, burned hands.

I'm very fortunate.

Stitches get removed. Bandages removed. Healing. Movement is natural. I wake up one day and I feel like myself. Bertha is glad when I inform her. She smiles. We hug. Kiss. Have sweaty sex. She now sleeps in granny panties and a bra. I never saw her in a pair of granny panties. Didn't know she owned a pair. I've been through her panty drawer. She's still slightly disappointed in me.

I'll fix this Bertha.

I get Wendy to drive me to the police station. I tell her it's extremely important. It'll save me and Bertha's relationship. She laughs. Obliges.

She loves me.

I'm questioned and questioned and questioned the whole ride there. I just tell her it's to make Bertha happy. It's actually to make me happy. I admire her figure during the whole ride.

She lets me off a block away. We both know that's a good idea. I tell her to wait here. I shouldn't be long. I give her a hug longer than needed. Thanks Wendy. These ladies are goddesses. I forgot how much I loved my life. I almost accepted death. Now focus Donovan.

I'm stuck in line.

Ticket complaints.

I need this officer. I need that officer.

My asshole neighbor knocked over my mailbox.

That little piece of shit William down the street shit in my garden.

I need a restraining order against my husband. He smacks me around when dinner isn't ready once he returns home from work. Look at my fucking face.

This crazy old man thinks it's ok to look through my window at night. I like to sleep naked. I want him arrested. I think he's recording me.

Five more complaints to go. I try to stay patient.

Why would you beat your wife? She's supposed to be the most important woman in your life other than your mother.

My food isn't ready?

Smack.

Backtalk?

Smack.

You don't want to make love to me?

Smack.

The store didn't have my beer?

Smack.

My team lost?

Smack.

I lost my life savings on a stupid bet?

Smack.

My nine to five minimum wage job is the best I can do?

Smack.

I can barely provide for my family?

Smack.

I drink too much?

Smack.

I hate my life?

Smack.

I'll never hit Betha. You don't destroy art. You don't harm a goddess.

I go over to the lady as she's sitting down, filling out

paperwork. Her beauty is contaminated with a black eye, bruised jaw, and busted lip. She's broken.

I hate her husband.

She's wearing a sweat suit two sizes too large. I cannot tell her shape. Her face tells me she's in shape. She's voluptuous up top. I can see that even with the oversized sweat suit. I tell her she doesn't need her piece of shit husband.

"You sound like my mom."

"You don't."

"And what? Leave?"

"Yes."

"So just pack up and leave? Take our four kids? I have no job. I didn't ask for this life." She continues to fill out a form.

"Go live with your mom."

She laughs. "Yeah. Okay. And be ridiculed day in and day out. Donna I told you not to marry him. I told you not to quit school for that asshole. I told you he'll keep hitting you. I need a new life. That's what I need. Living with my mom is not an option. You got another option?"

"Kill him."

"You know this is a police station right?"

"Yes."

"And I told you I have four kids. I don't want to go to jail."

"I can do it."

Laughter.

I'm such a joke to everyone. I should be a comedian.

"That's sweet. But stupid me still loves my abusive husband. What's your name?"

"Donovan."

"Well Donovan as you can see I'm in a shitty situation." Her sadness grows.

"If he ever hurts you again poison him. Put lead flakes in his food. You are beautiful. You don't hurt beautiful. Slowly cut his brake line so he dies on the highway."

"I'll take a mental note of that. Thank you. If only I met someone like you sooner in life."

"They're better options Donna. Millions of them."

"I know. Thanks, but I can't leave. I just can't." Her voice cracks. "I have to finish this report. I hate paperwork. I'm not even sure I want to fill this out. I don't know what I'm doing with my life anymore."

Feelings are a curse. Feelings cause pain.

Life causes pain.

Everything causes pain.

I've lost my spot in line. I head to the back of the line. I'm the thirteenth person with a concern or issue. This is going to be a while. I hope Wendy doesn't leave. I pass the time thinking about the various ways of killing Donna's husband. There's a ton.

"What do you need."

"Do you know this one officer?"

"I know many. Be a little more specific son."

"My name is Donovan."

"What?"

"My name is Donovan Black."

"Why are you telling me your name? I didn't ask for your name. I asked for the officer's name."

Forget it.

What was his name? Fuck. "I don't remember."

"Then I cannot help you. Next."

Think Donovan.

I remember something.

"Wait. He has three kids. Two girls. A son named Billy."

Please work.

"Oh. You need Officer Rossi." His face changes to expressing disappointment. "Jesus Christ what did Rossi do now. He didn't hit a kid again? Sorry but he's not here. He's suspended. Why do you want him?"

"Why did he get suspended?"

"I just said. He hit a kid. Why do you want him? He hit you? He hit someone you know?"

"I want to thank him." I lie. "He helped me."

"You sure you're talking about Rossi? I can't stand the guy. He's the reason cops get a bad rap. What he do for you?"

Think Donovan. "He stopped someone from robbing me. I forgot to thank him."

"When he do that?"

"A few weeks ago."

"And you want to thank him now?"

"Yes."

"Why?"

"I don't know. Do you know where he lives?"

"He'll be back in two weeks. Come back then."

"I've waited too long. I don't want him to forget me. I don't want him to forget how much he helped me."

"Okay. Sure. It's not my address. I'll write it down for you. Maybe if he sees someone give their appreciation to him he'll stop giving us a bad name. Maybe he'll stop abusing his power. I don't like the guy. I wish he was fired."

I don't like him either.

I take the paper with officer Rossi's address and leave.

My plan was never to meet Officer Rossi face to face at the police station. It was to somehow find out where he lives. Find out his license plate number. Use that to find his address. Figure out his full name. Search him online. Hopefully his house is in one of his photos. Somehow stalk him at work. Each day find out what additional street he uses to return home. I didn't expect it to be this easy. It shouldn't be that easy to get a police officer's address. That officer must really not like Officer Rossi.

I don't either.

Thanks.

I ask Wendy to take me to the address on the slip of paper. She says no. She has to work. Why Donovan?

Just because. No reason.

There is a reason. She's not going to give me a ride. That's unfortunate.

She wants to see the address. No. You won't give me

a ride there. What's the point when you won't give me a ride? She tells me I better not hurt her sister again. I already know that Wendy. She's surprised I'm still alive. Bertha must really love you. I know Wendy. I know.

She takes me home.

I offer my services to Wendy for pleasure before she leaves. No, she says. I have to hurry and shower. Let me shower with you then. She smiles. You'll make me late. Next time I take one you can join.

I think you told me that before.

The house becomes empty. Bertha is nowhere to be found.

I log into the laptop and search the address online. An hour and twenty-four minute walk to Officer Rossi's house. I don't mind walking. I'll make the walk worth it. Excitement builds inside. You brought me pain Officer Rossi.

Now you'll bring me pleasure.

18

Cell phone jammers block signals between a cellular device and the cell tower. They're used in prisons. Criminals don't deserve the luxury of using a cell phone. Jammers are banned in some countries and states. They can be disguised as everyday household objects.

Lamp? Cell phone jammer. That bottle of wine that never gets touched at your grandparent's house during thanksgiving? Cell phone jammer. No wonder your phone never works over there during the holidays. Grandma just wants you to talk to her once a year. Random pack of cigarettes that has a wire connected to a wall outlet. Yup. Cell phone jammer.

Once my teacher in high school used a jammer during his classes. Said we are doing too well on his exams. Blamed our electronic encyclopedias for our success. Grades suffered. No one studied. No one cared. It was a stupid class. He ended up losing his job. He was an asshole anyway.

I ordered one a few days ago. Just got it in the mail. Express shipping. Delivered in a plain white box. Didn't have it sent to this house. I picked a house down the street with an old lady that occupied the place. Old ladies like to talk. Mrs. Graham does.

Mrs. Linda Graham. Seventy-three years young. Old. Lives alone. Her three sons don't visit much. She's misses them. Poor old lady.

We became close. Sure I'll stop by again and talk. Sure I'll be your friend. You're right. Your children should visit you more often. Your neighbors are weird. Yes they are. Sure I'll go grocery shopping for you. No problem. Thanks for letting a perfect stranger use your age old computer and credit card and order a cell phone jammer from China. Thanks Mrs. Linda Graham.

It has a range of one square mile. That'll be enough I hope. I hope it's not a cheap Chinese piece of shit. I should have done more research.

I'm too excited.

I bought a hog mask. The costume store out of town didn't have a pig mask. Guy told me they were out. Said they ran out a few days ago. Unfortunate.

I kept asking Wendy to give me a ride there for days but she kept giving me excuse after excuse. Donovan I gotta go to work. Donovan I'm tired. Donovan it's six in the morning. I'm meeting someone today. My leg hurts. Give me a back massage then I'll consider it. You should definitely work on your back massages Donovan. Bertha needs me to take her to a few places today. Sorry Donovan. Maybe tomorrow.

I should have just bought one online. Oh well. A hog mask will do.

I convinced Wendy to take me to the hardware store after the costume store. I bought a machete with Mrs. Graham's credit card. The back of the blade is serrated in case you want to saw wood.

Cool.

I don't tell Wendy what's in the bag when she asks. It's a secret I tell her. She doesn't seem to care.

I don't think I'll see Mrs. Graham anymore. I gave her card back. Said I forgot to return it the last time I got her groceries. I gave her a hug and told her I'll see her tomorrow.

I won't.

Poor old lady.

I won't miss her smell.

She smelled old, expiring.

I wake up someday later. Bertha is sleeping naked.

Finally. It took her long enough. Unnatural beauty. I love it. I rub and kiss on her round assets, trying not to wake her. No sex for me this morning. Today is the day. A different type of pleasure, enjoyment, rush, is needed today. I need Bertha asleep.

It's early. It's the weekend. I grab my machete, jammer, and hog mask, put them in a book bag I stole from the old lady's house, and head for the front door. Wendy is not up and about yet. Great. I leave the house.

This walk sucks. It's hot outside. I hope Officer Rossi has air conditioning in his home. My sweaty fingers are ruining this paper I printed with directions to that pig's house. I should have brought a water bottle. Focus on the reward Donovan. Sweat gets in my eyes.

I really should have brought water. I still have about thirty minutes to go. I need water. I stop at a house with a navy blue door and knock. A kid answers. He's wearing a red cape. Another hero? I wonder if he knew that kid I knew. What was that kid's name? Doesn't matter. He's dead.

"Can you please bring me some water."

"I'm not allowed to talk to strangers."

"You just talked to me."

"I'm going to tell my dad."

"No. Wait. Get me some water and I'll give you a dollar."

"Five."

"What? No."

"My dad told me strangers are bad."

"But you asked a stranger for five dollars."

"I don't like you. Your face looks funny."

I don't like you either shithead. "Okay get me some water and I'll give you ten bucks."

His face lights up. He gets the water. I drink the water. Thanks shithead.

"Where is the ten bucks?"

"Never trust strangers shit boy."

I leave. Valuable lesson you just learned kid.

I'm here. There isn't a car in the driveway. It's probably in their garage. They probably don't have a car. Bertha and Wendy's house is bigger. A slight, enjoyable rage starts to build inside my body. I'm going to enjoy this. Get to work Donovan.

I find a place to hide in the back of the house. Their backyard is fenced. I almost broke my neck climbing over. Be more careful Donovan. Their back door is open. What is wrong with people. Bad people exist in the world.

There is a wall outlet outside the house. I plug up the cell phone jammer. No calls for help will be made. Remember to cut the landlines once you're in the house Donovan. I didn't even test to see if this jammer works.

I'm just outside the backdoor crouched. It leads to an empty laundry room. The washer and dryer are off. I enter. Another door leads to a kitchen. It's cracked a little. I can see a lady through the glass. I guess Officer Rossi's wife. She'll tell me where her pig for a husband is. I pull my machete out. I put on the hog mask.

I pounce.

The serrated back of the blade presses against her neck. I'm not going to hurt her. I can't hurt a woman. I want to hurt her pig. She stutters asking me what I want.

"Where is Officer Rossi?"

"Al is not ho- home. Please," She continues to stutter. "I have ki- kids. They're sleeping. Don't hurt us."

She's scared.

I'm happy.

"When will he be back?"

"An hour. Maybe two." She starts crying.

I forgot rope. "Do you have rope. I forgot to buy some."

"No."

"Don't lie to me lady. I will cut your head clean off." I lie.

"Please don't! I have kids."

I don't give a shit. "What do you have?"

"Only sewing string."

"Shit. I should have planned more. Sorry lady. It's not your fault. I should have thought about this day more. That's saying a lot because I thought about this day a lot. You gotta have something better than sewing string. You're becoming useless. Your body is starting to not need your head anymore."

"Al keeps zip ties in the drawer over there."

Al is a monster. I'm going to kill that pig.

"Now that'll work."

I bring her with me to the drawer and make her grab the zip ties. I zip tie her hands behind her back and tie her legs together by her feet. I then zip tie her hands and feet together behind her. I ask where are all the land lines. She tells me there is only one in the living room. I press the machete into her chest. Don't lie to me lady. She tells me she isn't. I leave her in the kitchen.

She wasn't lying. I checked and double checked to make sure, tying up her kids upstairs with zip ties during the process. Kids don't fight much when you wave a machete in front of their face.

I'm shaking in excitement.

I'm back in the kitchen. I had to drag the wife back into the kitchen. She was in the hallway.

Women.

She's not scared enough. I want her hyperventilating. I want her hysterical. I want her to go insane. I got an idea.

I grab the biggest four pots in the kitchen. They're now boiling water on top of the stove. I tell her I'm going to boil her two daughter's bodies and bake her son in the oven. I tell her little girls taste better boiled. Little boys taste better baked. I guess that is what a psycho says. I wouldn't know.

Her pleas for me to stop this gets a little hysterical. Telling a mother that I'm going to cook her children, I thought, would result in a more animated reaction. I'm enjoying it. This is a good build up. My heart pounding is music to my ears.

I set the oven to five hundred degrees.

I drag the wife down the steps. I left multiple notes in the laundry room, kitchen, front door, and living room informing Officer Rossi his wife is with a pig in the basement. I ask the wife where are all the guns located in the house. She said there are two guns, maybe one, depending if her pig husband took one out with him that are located under each of their pillows. They kinda sleep with a gun to their head. I ask are they loaded. She cries yes. They're prepared for people like me but they weren't prepared today. I blame the husband. He's a piece of shit. The wife and kids seem fine. The son needs basketball lessons.

I notice the wife has a small chest. What a shame. No wonder I'm being such a dick to her.

There are two guns, one under each pillow. That's unfortunate Officer Rossi. You're going to have to fight me bare handed. Bare hands versus a machete. I'll take my chances.

The magazines are thrown in one boiling pot of water. A cell phone I guess belongs to the wife also goes into boiling water. The guns, knives, forks, and all the rest of the sharp items I can find are thrown into the oven. I want a fair fight.

There are a pair of black gloves lying next to the stove. I tossed them in one of the pots of boiling water. I thank God Officer Rossi forgot those gloves that night.

The little things in life.

Once back in the basement I inform the wife that I'm going to go upstairs to each of her children's room, chop them up and cook them in the various ways said earlier. I tell her the younger the meat the more tender and flavorful. Little boys taste better than little girls. I tell her I wish she had more than one son. It's going to take a while to eat her daughters.

All lies.

Now she's the hysterical I was looking for. The flailing on the basement floor. The screaming. The snot running down her nose. The hyperventilating between pleas to not hurt her children. I'm not going to hurt them. She doesn't know that. A lie can be so painful. So powerful. I love this pain and hurt I'm causing.

Why are there so many different ways to say and describe pain? Hurt. Suffering. Agony. Pain is hurt. Hurt is pain. Pain is suffering. Suffering is pain. Pain is agony. Agony is pain. And there are even more words the same as pain. Why do we have to be so fancy with our descriptions. Pain is pain.

Stay focused Donovan.

The wife asks who am I. I tell her I'm a pig. You see my mask. It's a hog mask. It's supposed to be a pig mask. The store ran out of pig mask. I'm a cop. A dirty pig. Just like your husband. Get it?

Oink oink!

She tells me they have money. Just tell her a number. Why do they always offer money? It's not money I want I tell her. I just want to end her husband's life. He hurt me. No. He caused me a lot of pain. I must return the pain he caused. She wouldn't understand.

I head upstairs just to cause more pain to the wife. Her husband is the only person I want. Her kids will stay tied up, locked in their rooms. I don't hurt children.

There are multiple deadbolts on the inside of the basement door. I guess so Officer Rossi's family can hide in the basement if an intruder enters the home. Their panic room. Panic basement?

I don't know.

They must really care about safety. Well that backfired for Officer Rossi. Have fun trying to save your wife locked in the basement you dirty pig.

In the hallway I hear a door open from the front of the house. A few moments later Officer Rossi yells his wife's name. The tone of pain. The sound of horror and concern enter the air. Butterflies fly inside my stomach. Yes. It's finally time. I head back to the basement, locking all dead bolts. I'm steaming with excitement. I tell the lady her husband's home. She already knows. She's been screaming his name since I was locking the basement door.

It's finally time.

I thought about meeting him at whatever door he entered the house through, slicing and chopping up his body, but that wouldn't be enjoyable. He'll just experience a few moments of pain. Then death. That's not good enough. I want him to lose hope knowing that nothing he does today will save his family. I want him to believe his family will die today. He should have carried his gun with him. That is what this rotten pig deserves. He deserves to feel powerless. Useless. A waste of a life. I can't stop smiling behind this mask.

He bangs on the basement door demanding I open it. Not going to happen. Not yet.

I see duct tape on a table. I use it to silence her noises. I want to hear and enjoy all of Officer Rossi's sorrow.

Fucking pig.

He speaks.

"I'm a cop. There is no way you will come out on top."

"Eat shit pig."

"Who are you? What do you want with me and my family," Officer Rossi yells. "Connie I'm here baby. I'll get you out of this."

She can't reply pig. "I want your wife dead. And it's because of you Officer Rossi. You brought me pain. I just want to send some your way." I should have worked on what I was going to say.

"Who the hell are you?"

More banging on the door. It won't open. His security measures prevent it. The locks are supposed to keep me away from his wife but they keep him from her.

Ironic? I don't know.

"I'm the person that will be the end to your wife. Your marriage. Have fun being a single parent Officer Rossi." I slash around his wife, taking extra care not to hurt her, slicing boxes, bags, shelves, screaming occasionally, enjoying his curses and swears from behind the door.

The banging and yelling and demands stop. I think he leaves. I think he went for his guns. Have fun pulling them out of a five hundred degree oven if you can find them. He won't find them. Nobody bakes a gun.

Time passes. Screams and yells for why his cell phone doesn't work continue and continue. Promises are yelled to his children in front of locked doors, telling each child he'll save them after saving mommy first.

He's panicking. Check on the kids you idiot. I'm loving it. He doesn't know what to do. He must think I have the two guns. He doesn't know what to think. I control his pain. I control his thoughts. I control his family's future. His future. I'm his God. I'm their God. I feel so powerful. The control. I love it.

The wife starts talking. More pleas to stop this. More crying. More begging.

They are lost puppies. Confused puppies. I should have used more duct tape.

The banging returns. "Don't kill her. I'll give you whatever you want. Just don't hurt my wife."

I put more duct tape over the wife's mouth. I don't want her to ruin my lie. "Keep talking and I'll blow her fucking brains out man. I'm a sick fuck man."

I'm having too much fun.

"No. Take me instead."

"I want your wife dead. I always loved her. She was supposed to be mine. I watch her every day. She doesn't need you. She's mine. Those are supposed to be my kids. I'm supposed to be you. You stole my life."

Bullshit, bullshit, bullshit. Confusion, confusion, confusion. I want you to lose your fucking mind Officer Rossi.

You should have left me alone at the park you pig piece of shit.

"Who the hell are you? We can talk this out."

I'm the man you cannot escape in your dreams. I'm that silhouette in your mind. You probably don't remember my voice. The answer is in your head. I'm the picture you cannot remember. You'll find out who I am when it's too late.

I'm Donovan.

I want to turn this fun up a notch. I think of what Donovan can do. I know what I can do. Can I hurt a woman? Mentally? Sure. Physically? I don't know. Guess I'll find out.

I grab the wife. I tell her I'm going to release her hands. If you do anything stupid I'm going to kill you. Your children will be motherless. Then they'll be dead. Do you understand? She agrees.

I cut the zip ties. I tell her to close her eyes. Close your fucking eyes. She does. I can't believe someone can cry this much. Her husband yells some stuff but I'm zoning him out. I need to focus. I've never done this before. I pin her left hand to the ground. The machete separates her hand from her arm.

Groans burst the duct tape away, freeing her screams. Her face loses spirit. Her eyes stare into another world. Shock? It's like she's choking. My heart's pounding with greater intensity. It concerns me.

Breath Donovan. You never had a rush like this.

The next hand is separated. She's back. Yells of suffering. Blood staining the floor. I free her legs. I'm done with her I tell her. You're free.

Officer Rossi wants to know what the fuck I did to his wife. He'll find out. She struggles to her feet, noises of pain singing from her vocal cords. Fresh nubs for hands can do that.

She makes it up the steps. She fumbles with the locks. None will open. Silly lady. You left your hands down stairs. I think about bringing them upstairs for her. I laugh internally.

She tells her husband her hands are gone. I chopped

them off. His voice cracks. He apologizes to her. Says he'll get her out of this. She tells him to help her. She's scared.

Your husband can't save you. I can. Death can. I don't want you to die. I want you to suffer. I want you to lose hope. I want you to hunger for death. Lose hope lady. Beg for death. Pain is everlasting. Death brings an end. Accept death as your personal savior.

Officer Rossi yells. I hear him run away from the door. He returns moments later. He yells at his wife to go down the steps and hide. Fight Connie. Fight he yells.

I want no more parts of Connie. I never wanted any. I let her hide.

Something heavy smashes some dead bolts loose. A hammer? Another bang. No hammer. Something larger. Another smash puts a hole in the door.

A sledgehammer.

"I'm going to fucking kill you," Officer Rossi proclaims.

Oh shit.

I head towards the steps to end him but something jumps on my back. Teeth sink into my left trapezius. Sounds of pain leave my mouth. The machete drops.

No.

Teeth chomp into my right trap. I wrestle with the wife. She keeps fucking biting me. Blood is everywhere. Stop it you bitch. I manage to throw her off of me. I kick her in her fucking head.

Bitch.

Officer Rossi has opened the door. I can't lift my arms. My shoulders are on fire. My traps leak. Blood is leaking somewhere out of the back of my head. My neck aches from bites.

I manage to pick up the machete. Now it's time to suffer a warrior's death you fucking pig. I try to lift my arm. I forgot I can't. I try harder. Fuck the pain Donovan. This isn't good. It's pointless. Pain has found me again. Death is approaching me.

Death is Officer Rossi.

Rossi sprints down the steps, sledge hammer cocked, ready to make me nonexistent. I'm ready. I've had enough fun.

Bang.

Another bang.

Two gunshots. One in officer Rossi's back. Another in the back of officer Rossi's head. The pig falls dead at my feet.

I look up at the top of the steps. Bertha. She's crying. Her face displays anger.

Bertha?

Darkness.

I wake up getting dragged out of the pig's house in handcuffs. Not by cops. By Bertha and Wendy. I'm thrown into the back of a black van. Wendy and Bertha both don't own a black van.

Bertha sits across from me. Wendy sits next to me. Wendy looks the same. Her cheerful regular self. Bertha is a wreck. No make-up. She's only wearing sadness and tears on her face. Anger too. Disappointment.

We drive off.

I start to talk.

"Stop it Brown Bear. Don't you dare say a word."

I try again. I'm pistol whipped.

I thought she loved me.

"There was a lady down there with you Brown Bear. Her hands were cut off. I killed her. I can still smell her on you. I'm too hurt to ask what you were doing with her."

The only thing I can smell is blood. The back of my head feels different. My traps feel different. I feel drowsy.

"I told you Donovan. Stop hurting my sister," Wendy tells me.

Don't you think I already know that? "I'm sorry."

"Sorry isn't enough Brown Bear."

"Hey sweet cheeks."

Why is he here? Fucking Bianca. He's driving. Good. I

don't want to see his fucking face.

Now I know that different feeling. He stitched up my bites. Easy on the painkillers next time Bianca. Now I know why my brain is fuzzy.

"Do you even love Bertha Brown Bear?" Bianca asks.

I'm not answering that stupid fucking question.

"Answer him Brown Bear."

"You already know I do Bertha."

"Why were you down there with that woman."

"I wanted to kill her husband. He wasn't home. So I tormented his family until he got home. He was the one who beat me that night at the park. I wanted to show him the power I had over him. His life. His family. His mind. It was working until that lady started biting me."

Bertha gasps in disgust. "I'm the only one who can bite you."

Wendy chuckles.

"Don't you dare start Wendolynn." She points the gun at her sister.

"Okay. Relax Bertha."

What? How the fuck does Bertha's mind work? "She was trying to kill me." I explain.

"Sure she was."

"I chopped her fucking hands off."

"Don't curse at me."

"Sorry. I'm sorry."

I can't win with this woman.

She starts to break down even more, crying. I hate when she cries. She looks so ugly crying. "Why did you do this? You almost died."

"I love the rush it gives me."

Wendy shakes her head.

Bianca makes an annoyed sound.

Fuck you too Bianca.

Focus Donovan.

"I almost lost you."

"I know. I'm sorry."

"I have to punish you Brown Bear."

"I know. I know. Just tie me up again. I'm really sorry Bertha."

"No. That didn't work. I'm sending you to live with Bianca. She'll teach you some manners."

"What the fuck?" Oh God. Please no. "Please Bertha. Not him. Anyone else."

"Bianca is a woman. You're going to learn to respect her and me."

He's a phony. You don't respect phony.

"You'll respect Bianca. Do whatever she says and learn how to treat a woman during your time with her. I can't fathom that it has come to this between us Brown Bear." She drowns in her tears, sorrow.

I can't enjoy the parts of her body her clothes are revealing. I'm so mad.

One time when I was younger, I believe around the age of 13, I was over my mother's friend's house. I had a crush on the lady's older daughter. She had a younger daughter also. About five. I was sitting on the couch watching TV and the oldest sister fell asleep on the opposite couch. I sat next to her. She had large breasts. I fondled them in her sleep. I kissed her.

I've always wanted to. This was my best chance. Once in a lifetime opportunity. I dreamed about those breasts. I took extra care not to wake her. Both mothers were in the kitchen chatting, gossiping. Minutes passed. She stayed asleep. I was in paradise. I took it to the next level. She was wearing a dress. I felt under her dress. She moved. I panicked. I took a break. I liked the way her boobs felt more. Spend the rest of the time that I had on her boobs Donovan I told myself. This was amazing. I've waited so long for this. She started to wake up so I stopped. I started watching TV again.

I looked around and noticed that the little sister was staring at me crouched from the top of the steps. My heart sunk into my stomach. How long had she been there? I needed to know. My flesh grew hot. I ran up to the steps after the little sister. I needed to know what she saw. How much she saw. She ran and slammed her door. Locked it. I couldn't open it. I whispered to her that I just wanted to talk to her. I was panicking inside. I was losing my mind. How much did she see? I wanted to break that door down, crack that little girl's skull open, swim in her memories and erase what she saw. I was so lost. I was young. I just wanted to touch some breasts. How much did that little fucking girl see?

That's what I want to do now. Crack open Bertha's skull, swim around her mind, find all the pain, suffering, and confusion I caused her, and remove it. Find that part of her brain that never believes Donovan and remove it. She'll die but she won't ever know I ever hurt her. Poor Bertha. You'll always know what I've done to you. The pain I caused you. I could never kill you.

Fuck.

"I bought a crate Brown Bear."

"Why? We don't have a dog."

"For you. It's part of your puni-" Bertha drowns more into her sorrows. She's not even speaking English now. Some type of foreign, crying, sobbing speak.

"It's part of your punishment Donovan. Bertha bought a crate for you to sleep in and when you're bad during your stay with Bianca."

"It was my idea," Bianca states.

I'm lost for words.

This is serious.

"My sister is tired of being hurt Donovan. She killed all her other lovers. There is something special about you. None of her other lovers have lasted this long."

"I don't see what she sees in you Brown Bear."

"Just shut up and drive Bianca," Bertha shouts.

Thanks Bertha. Shut the fuck up Bianca. I go sit next to Bertha.

I try to lay my head on her. She pushes me off. I go to kiss her cheek. She goes to sit next to her sister.

"When will I see you again?"

"I… don't… *KNOOOOOW!* I'm so sorry Brown Bear. I have to do this. You were a bad Brown Bear."

This is serious. I don't like this at all. Is this really my future?

I'll rather be dead. Somebody please end me.

"Don't worry Bertha. You know I'll treat him right. I know he belongs to you."

All Bertha does it shake her head in agreement and cry, cry, cry.

Oh god.

"How did y'all find me?"

"That watch you're wearing. The one Bertha gave you. It's connected with Bertha's phone."

A jammer can't jam a signal to a digital watch? Stupid fucking jammer. Chinese piece of shit.

I start to get light headed.

"Please Bertha. You really going to make your Brown Bear live somewhere else? With someone else?"

"Pathetic."

All Bertha does is cry.

I'm starting to feel weird. My body is feeling foreign. Distant. My known future haunts me. I can't change it. I'm losing control.

Not again.

Stop it.

Bianca turns some music on.

White spots appear in my vision.

No.

More spots. Vision fading.

I can barely see Bertha.

No. Stop it Donovan.

Breathe.

I need water.

More spots paint over my reality. Erase my reality.
No!
"Please Bertha don't do this to m-"
Darkness.

I would like to thank you for reading my first novel *Oh Donovan*. I would love if you wouldn't mind talking about my novel online with the hashtag #OhDonovanNovel. It would be greatly appreciated. Don't forget to lookout for updates on my social media accounts for updates on what I'm writing next. You can also email me if you like. I'll love to hear what you thought of my novel.

I truly hope you enjoyed reading *Oh Donovan*.

Leonardo Collazo

Twitter: @Leocollazo43
Instagram: @Leocollazo43
SnapChat: Leothelion2747
Email: Leocollazo43@gmail.com
#OhDonovanNovel